MYSTERIOUS

K.M. SCOTT

BOOKS BY K.M. SCOTT

Crash Into Me (Heart of Stone #1)

Fall Into Me (Heart of Stone #2)

Give In To Me (Heart of Stone #3)

Heart of Stone Volume One

Ever After (Heart of Stone #4)

A Heart of Stone Christmas (Heart of Stone #5)

Return To Me (Heart of Stone #6)

Forever With Me (Heart of Stone #7)

Heart of Stone Volume Two

Hard As Stone (Heart of Stone #8)

Set In Stone (Heart of Stone #9)

Silent As A Stone (Heart of Stone #10)

Heart of Stone Volume Three

All of Me (Heart of Stone #11)

Temptation (Club X #1)

Surrender (Club X #2)

Possession (Club X #3)

Satisfaction (Club X #4)

Acceptance (Club X #5)

Complete Club X Series Paperback

Dirty Boss Volume One

BOOKS BY K.M. SCOTT WRITING AS GABRIELLE BISSET

Blood Avenged (Sons of Navarus #1)

Blood Betrayed (Sons of Navarus #2)

Blood Spirit (Sons of Navarus #3)

Blood Prophecy (Sons of Navarus #4)

Blood Craving (Sons of Navarus #5)

Blood Eclipse (Sons of Navarus #6)

Blood Ascendant (Sons of Navarus #7)

Stolen Destiny (Destined Ones Duet #1)

Destiny Redeemed (Destined Ones Duet #2)

Love's Master

Masquerade

The Victorian Erotic Romance Trilogy

MYSTERIOUS

From *New York Times* bestselling author K.M. Scott comes a sexy opposites attract romance about two people who couldn't be more different yet couldn't be more right for one another.

Liam and Mia can't help but be explosive when they get together, but no matter what happens, he never forgets his job is to keep her safe. Every day, that gets harder and harder, but now that Liam loves Mia, nothing will get in his way of being the protector she needs.

Unfortunately, there are those behind the scenes who have different plans for the new couple, friends and enemies with their own agendas.

They're about to find out that once a man like Liam Jackson falls for a woman, he'll move heaven and earth to keep her safe.

No matter what he has to do.

Published in the United States

ISBN: 978-1-955335-08-9

CHAPTER ONE

iam

SLOWLY, I OPEN MY EYES AND SEE NOTHING BUT white. Definitely not my bedroom. I try to place where I might be, but nothing makes sense. What is that sound? It's a constant beeping, but I can't figure out where it's coming from.

My phone? No. Maybe my alarm? No, I'd never choose to wake up to that noise.

I look left and right, but I see no one in this room with me. Did I change my bedroom to all white? No, that doesn't sound like anything I'd do. I hate all white rooms. They feel so sterile, so much like hospital rooms.

Then I remember I would be in my room at Mia's house. No, that doesn't make sense either because that

1

room isn't all white. What color is that room? Tan? Beige?

Whatever color it is, I'm not there.

The memory of Mia running into traffic flashes through my brain, and panic rushes through me. Did she get hit by a car? Is she okay?

I sit up to get out of bed, and instantly, pain stabs down my entire right side. Fuck! What the hell is that? Turning to look at my arm, I see it wrapped in bandages and wires all around me.

Awake after feeling like someone sunk a knife into my skin, I finally understand where I am. That explains the wires and the beeping.

But why am I in a hospital?

"Please remain still, Mr. Jackson. You've suffered a gunshot wound to your arm, so we need you to keep still so you don't tear any of the stitches. The doctor will be in momentarily," a woman's voice says, and I turn my head to see a tall nurse with the palest skin I've ever encountered smiling down at me.

"Where is Mia?" I ask, desperate to know she didn't get shot too.

Jesus, if the bastard who got me got her too, I'll never forgive myself.

"Mia?" the nurse asks like she's doesn't understand the question.

Nodding, I answer, "Yeah. Singer. Superstar. She should have been with me when I was brought here."

God, I hope she was. The memory of her running away floods my mind, and all I can think of is Mia off on her own up to who knows what. Or worse, hurt by the son of a bitch who shot me and pulled over on some road bleeding to death.

The nurse's eyes open wide, and she smiles. "Oh, the young woman who rode in with you on the ambulance. Yes, she's here. She's been here the whole time. I'm sure she'll be thrilled to hear that you're finally awake."

"So she's okay?" I ask, suddenly fearful she needed to be in the ambulance like I did.

The nurse nods as I notice her nametag that reads Theresa. "She's okay, even if she is a little impatient. I'm going to assume she was just frightened that you might not make it."

I notice a hint of unhappiness filling the woman's voice as she says that first sentence. Knowing Mia, she had some kind of temper tantrum when she couldn't force them to make me better on her schedule instead of theirs.

"If I'm not mistaken, you have an entire waiting room full of people very eager to see you. As soon as the doctor comes in and takes a look at you, we can bring some of them in."

My mind fills with the image of my family out there scared to death I might not make it. Not my father, of course, since he's always of the belief that we Jacksons are indestructible, but I know my mother and she's let herself worry that the last time we talked at my grandmother's house that day when she convinced me to take the job with Mia was, in fact, the very last time she'd ever hear my voice.

Abbi Jackson is nothing if not an overreacting mother when it comes to me.

"Okay, thanks. I'm sure they're just frightened. It's not every day that you hear someone you know got shot," I say, preemptively hoping to excuse whatever madness my family has brought to the hospital while I've been in here.

Just as those words leave my lips, I hear Mia arguing with someone right outside in the hallway. "I don't care what the rules are. I need to see him. He's the person in charge of my security. Where he goes, I go, and vice versa, so please move so I can get in there to see him."

I glance up at the nurse as she turns to leave the room. "I'm sure she's just scared. If you send her in, I can calm her down and probably make things better for all involved," I say sheepishly.

For a moment, Theresa doesn't seem too inclined to give in and break whatever rule there is that says I can't have visitors before the doctor sees me, but as Mia continues to berate someone out in the hallway, actually threatening the poor soul if they don't let her in, the nurse with the pale skin gives in.

"Just as long as she doesn't upset you."

With a smile, I shake my head. "She's just someone you have to get used to. Once you know who she really is, Mia's a lot easier to deal with. I promise she won't upset me."

As the nurse leaves, I think I hear her grumble under her breath something about Mia upsetting everyone else on the entire floor for the past two hours. That sounds like her.

A few seconds later, the woman herself rushes into the room and stops dead at the foot of my bed. Staring at me with horror in her eyes, she shakes her head before starting to cry.

"They wouldn't let me in until right now. What kind of place is this? A person gets shot protecting someone, and then they don't let the person you were protecting in to see you? I didn't know if you were dead or what might have happened, Liam. These people are monsters! I hate them for letting me think all those horrible things all alone out there."

"I don't think they meant to scare you. They had to focus on making sure the bullet didn't do any huge damage. At least that's what I assume all these wires and machines are about."

The horror in her eyes transfers to the rest of her expression when she looks up and sees what's commonplace in a hospital room all around me. "Oh, my God! Did you have to be on life support? What are all these machines doing here? Oh, Liam, it's bad, isn't it? You got shot because of me, and now you're going to be laid up for God only knows how long."

I hold my good hand up to stop her before she completely unravels. Thank God I have experience with a mother who overreacts or dealing with Mia right now might be too much to handle.

"It's going to be fine. It's not like I'm actually on anything to help me breathe or anything like that.

These machines are standard in most hospitals. It doesn't mean I'm dying or anything."

Mia stares at the wall behind me for a long moment before returning her attention to me. "You're really going to be okay? You're not just lying to me to shut me up?"

With a smile, I shake my head. "Well…"

Hurt replaces fear in her expression, so I quickly add, "I'm not lying, but you have to be nicer to everyone here, Mia. They're just doing their jobs. They have rules about visitors, especially when someone's not conscious yet. That's why they didn't let you in to see me before. Take it easy on them. They're fixing me up, so I'll be fine. Don't you worry."

"Do you promise?"

For the first time since she barged into my hospital room, I see real sadness in her eyes. I don't want her to feel that way, so I quickly smile as broadly as I can and hope she sees I'm going to be okay.

"I promise. You aren't going to get rid of me that easily."

And in a flash, whatever happiness she felt when I said I promise disappears. Tears well in her eyes, and then she covers her face with her hands and sobs, "This is all my fault. You would have never been there to get shot if it wasn't for me trying to leave the estate without any bodyguards. I'm so sorry, Liam. I wasn't trying to get rid of you. That's not what I wanted at all."

"It's okay, Mia. This isn't your fault, so don't think that way. Whatever happened, I'm going to be fine."

Just as I hope I'm convincing her, the doctor comes in and looks at Mia still crying at the foot of my bed. "He's going to be fine, miss."

Mia drops her hands and sniffles as she stares up at him with genuine hope in her eyes. "He is? Really?"

"Really," the man says as I try to figure out if he's old looking with dyed dark brown hair or just someone who's spent too much time out in the sun and has the deep wrinkles in his face to prove it.

"Okay," she says, wiping tears from her cheeks. "Because he's very important to me. I need him to be one hundred percent or I can't do what I need to do, which will mean a lot of people will be unhappy."

He seems confused by her explanation for a few seconds, but then a look of appreciation comes over him and he nods like he finally understands what she's talking about. "You're Mia, the singer! My wife loves your music. We played one of your songs for our dance at our wedding reception."

The center of his attention, she beams her happiness at being recognized. "I'm so happy to hear that. So you see, I need Liam to be able to go out on tour, and if he can't go, I can't go, so I need him to go or thousands upon thousands of fans are going to be disappointed every night when I have to cancel my tour."

My doctor turns to look over at me, but I have nothing to add. Mia seems to believe she can't go out on tour without me, so I'm just going to have to be well enough to do my job so she can do hers.

"So Mr. Jackson, you seem very important to this

young woman. I've taken a look at your injury and it wasn't too bad. You bled a lot, which probably made it look worse than it was, but I was able to sew you up with no problem. The bullet exited out the back of your arm, so you have stitches on both sides, but that's it."

I push myself up so I'm sitting instead of lying down and smile at the good news. "Great! See, Mia? No problem."

"But I do want your right arm in a sling so you have the least amount of movement possible for at least three weeks. Other than that, you can resume whatever your duties are."

Quickly, Mia explains, "Liam is my bodyguard. He's essential to my being able to perform, so just hearing you say he's going to be okay is the best news ever!"

"Well, he's going to be fine, so let the show go on."

The nurse who left just before the doctor showed up pokes her head into the room and asks, "Can Mr. Jackson see his family? They're out here very worried about him."

No doubt my mother has pestered every person at the nurses' station since the minute she walked into the building. It's my broken wrist in third grade all over again.

"If the patient is up for it, I'm fine with him having visitors. I'm going to get the process moving to get you released, but until then, you'll be in a holding pattern for a little while, so enjoy the visit from your family."

"Thanks, Doc."

CHAPTER TWO

iam

When he and the nurse leave, Mia rushes over to the right side of my bed. "Does this mean I get to meet the people in that picture you showed me?"

"I think so. I'm guessing at the very least my mother and father are out there, although the nurse mentioned something about the waiting room being full of my family, so some of the cousins and aunts and uncles might have come too. My mother probably made my injury sound way more serious than it actually was."

Gently pressing her palm to my chest, Mia shakes her head. "It was very serious, Liam. You got shot. Somebody put a bullet into your body. I don't care what that doctor said about it looking worse than it actually was. It was terrible. I thought you were going to die right there on the street. I don't ever want to feel that way again."

For the first time since I met her all those weeks ago, she sounds like she was genuinely concerned about me. Now as I look at her, it's hard to see the petulant client and the overwrought woman I chased into the street last night.

I cover her hand with mine and sigh, knowing I shouldn't be touching her like this, not even to show my kindness and gratitude for getting the ambulance to take care of me. Mia is the woman I protect. We're not supposed to be anything more.

The problem is it's clear to me that we both know we are something more than merely client and bodyguard.

With a gentle smile, she says, "I'm just so happy you're going to be okay."

Before I can respond, my mother, father, and Wilder come walking into the room, and I immediately see my mother's a mess. Her eyes are red like she's been crying, and her cheeks are all flushed.

"Liam! Honey, the nurse just told us you're going to be okay. I was so worried. When we got the call that you'd been shot, I felt like I was going to pass out right there in the kitchen," my mother says breathlessly.

She never disappoints when it comes to being emotional about her children.

"I'm fine, Mom. Honestly."

Hoping to direct the attention away from my

injury, I smile and say, "Everyone, this is Mia. The woman I work for."

The way the words come out sound odd, like I'm trying to hide something, but none of them were a lie. I do work to protect her. That I don't want to share with anyone, including Mia, how I feel about her isn't a lie.

Well, maybe a sin of omission.

My family members all look over at Mia in unison as if they rehearsed the move, and I see my father raise a single eyebrow before looking back at me. I know what he's thinking. It's written all over his face.

What's written all over my mother's face is utter adoration. "Oh, it's so nice to meet you!" she gushes. "I've seen your picture a million times, but you're so much more beautiful in person."

"The same with me, Mrs. Jackson. When Liam showed me the picture of you and your husband, I thought you were so pretty, but in person, you're just stunning. I guess that teaches us not to believe what the media shows us," Mia says sweetly, instantly charming my mother with her compliment.

Patting under her eyes, she says, "Oh, thank you. That's so nice of you. I was worried I looked terrible after crying so much. I was so scared when we found out Liam had been shot."

As they enjoy their mutual admiration society, my father asks, "So do you know who shot you?"

Typical Kane Jackson. He noticed how beautiful Mia was and where her hand was on my chest, and then he immediately moved to wanting to know the details of the crime.

I shake my head, wishing I did know who the son of a bitch was who thought it was okay to take a shot at me. Assuming it was me he was aiming at, of course. I can't be sure of that yet, but I'll find out who did this to me. That's a given.

"No idea. We were downtown and there was some traffic, so I didn't notice anyone odd and certainly no one aiming a gun at me."

My father frowns and lets out a heavy sigh. "I hope the police find this person quickly."

Interrupting all this seriousness, Wilder walks around the side of my bed and sits down in the chair to my left. "So does this mean you'll be coming back to your place sooner than you expected?"

I look over at him and roll my eyes. "No."

Mia adds, "I need Liam to be my head of security for my upcoming tour, so he's going to be working for me for a while."

Her information clearly makes Wilder's day, if his grin is any indication. "Good to know."

Leave it to my brother to use a visit to see me after getting shot as a way to figure out how much longer he'll get to have my condo all to himself. Not that I think he's ever alone there. Something tells me he's living it up at my place, probably having parties every night of the week.

My parents shoot him a look of disapproval before turning their attention back to me. "I'm so happy your job is going well," my mother says and then adds, "other than getting shot, that is."

I can never tell if my mother is just subtly funny or off the wall bizarre when she says things like that. My father turns to look at her like he's sure it's the second option, but he's so used to her being like this that he simply shakes his head.

"What your mother means is it's clear you and Mia have cultivated a good working relationship. Most employers don't sit by the bedside of someone who works for them."

"Yes, that's exactly what I meant," my mother says, blushing.

It's all very strange and makes me wish Mia had moved her hand before they walked in, but still she keeps it resting on my chest. I'm sure my family thinks we're involved romantically, which isn't true.

At least not yet. Not really.

I glance over at her to see she has no idea anyone is paying attention to where she's touching me. Letting my gaze drop to her hand on my chest, I smile when I lift my eyes to look at her.

Finally, she understands what I'm trying hard to say without saying any words. Yanking her hand back into her body, she stands up quickly, clearly uncomfortable.

"I'm going to go talk to whoever is in charge to see why you haven't been discharged yet. I think I need to talk to the people who send the bill too since I don't want you to have to pay for this. It was very nice to meet all of you."

"Mia, I have insurance, so you don't have to worry," I say, but it's no use.

She shakes her head, frowning back at me. "No, you were shot doing something for me. I'll take care of it."

The four of us watch her hurry out of the room, and when she's gone, my mother says, "What's it like to have a superstar be a fan of yours?"

And there it is. At least I didn't have to wait long before one of them said something.

"It's not like that," I say, utterly unconvincingly. Even I don't believe what I'm saying.

"You may not think so, but she does," my mother says with a knowing smile as she looks over at my father nodding his agreement. "I'm not the only one who saw how much that girl cares for you, honey."

"I think you definitely have a fan, Liam," my father says with a twinkle in his eye.

"Seriously, guys, it's not like that. She's just upset because she saw me get shot. It's nothing more. Don't make a big deal out of this. Please?"

Wilder taps on my left forearm, and I turn to see him wearing a shit-eating grin. "If Grandma was here, you know what she'd be saying? You're protesting too much."

I shake my head and roll my eyes. "Nice butchering Shakespeare there, man. And I'm not protesting, so all of you stop it. I have to work with this woman. Don't make it weird."

"Nobody's making it weird, honey. We're just

telling you what's obvious to everyone," my mother says sweetly.

"Well, stop mentioning it. Maybe we can focus on the fact that I got shot. How about that?"

As soon as the words leave my mouth, I know I said the wrong thing. My mother's face contorts into an expression of pure sadness, and it looks like at any second, she's going to start crying.

My father throws me a dirty look, just to reinforce my knowledge that I screwed up, so I quickly say, "But I'm going to be fine. Just some stitches. Nothing else. I mean, they wouldn't let me out of the hospital if I was in bad shape, would they?"

A muted happiness returns to my mother's face, so at least that's something. Of course, she's never more thrilled than when she thinks I've met The One. That's how she refers to every woman I've gotten into a relationship with for the past five years. The One. They never are that one single soul who I want to spend the rest of my life with, but hope forever springs eternal in Abbi Jackson's motherly mind.

"Will you be able to return to your job?" my father asks in his typical no-nonsense fashion.

I nod, happy to be talking about something other than Mia and how the two of us feel about one another. "Absolutely. She's got a tour coming up, and I need to be there to make sure at every city she stops in that there's the right kind of security. You should have seen what they used to do for her. The biggest new star in the music world and I swear they used to cross their fingers and hope everything would work out.

She's lucky she didn't get kidnapped or worse with what her former head of security used to do."

"She's lucky to have you then," my father says with a smile I know means he wants to bust my ass about how I'm breaking my number one rule I've always followed in my business.

Never get close to the client.

A nurse thankfully ends any chance of that conversation occurring when she walks into the room with papers for me to sign. My family takes that as their cue to leave and come around to where Wilder has been sitting.

Leaning down, my mother presses a kiss to my cheek. "Please be careful, honey. I worry about you, and this only makes me more worried."

I smile up at her and see in her blue eyes she isn't exaggerating about her concern. "It's okay, Mom. I'll be fine."

"I love you, honey. Call more often so I can hear how things are going once you go out on the road with Mia, okay?"

My father nods, chiming in with his request for me to call home more than once in a while too. "Your mother's right. We want to hear all about it."

"I will. I promise."

After she gives me another kiss, my mother tousles my hair that's technically too short to mess up these days. "Good. Parents like to hear from their kids, even when they're grown men. Stay safe, honey. Okay? We love you, Liam."

My father simply smiles in that way that tells me

he thinks he knows much more about what's going on with Mia and me than I'm admitting. "Have fun."

They turn to leave and Wilder taps me on the arm again. "Don't worry about your place. It's in tip-top shape. Just as you left it. But you won't need that once you and Mia get together, right? Because I'm thinking we might as well keep it in the family if you don't."

Typical Wilder.

I look over at the nurse trying not to smile at my brother's awkward attempt at making me promise he can have my apartment now and point toward the door. "Out! And keep my place in good shape for when I get back. Got it?"

My brother waves off my comments with a chuckle on his way out the door. "Yeah, yeah. I know what I saw, so just remember the whole keeping it in the family idea. And call your mother, Liam. You know how she worries."

The nurse points to where I need to sign on half a dozen forms. Feeling the need to explain all she's heard, I say, "That's just my family. You know how family can be."

"You seem to have a lot of people who care about you, including that young woman out at the nurses' station. You're a lucky man, Mr. Jackson."

The look in her eyes tells me she thinks just like my family does. That Mia and I are involved. I guess there's no point in protesting. They're going to believe what they want to believe.

But I can't deny something's different between us now. I just don't know what to do about that.

CHAPTER THREE

ia

I SIT ON THE EDGE OF LIAM'S BED AS THE STAFF bring in anything he could possibly want while he rests like the doctor at the hospital said he needs to if I want him to be able to accompany me on the tour. I made them buy every magazine a man could want from the bookstore, and Cecelia made sure to buy all of his favorite food after I insisted he make me a list so he can have whatever he wants as he gets better.

When the guys finish lugging in a mini fridge so he doesn't have to do anything to have a drink whenever he wants, we're left alone for the first time since those few precious moments we had together in the hospital. Damn that nurse who couldn't give us just a minute more.

"If you get hungry, Cecelia has strict instructions

to make you whatever you ask for. All you have to do is tell her what you want. I gave her the list you wrote down, so she has everything you need. And if I have to hire a different chef to make something she can't make, then I'll do that."

Liam shakes his head, like he's embarrassed by all this attention he's getting. "You don't have to do all of this. I'm fine, Mia. Just a few stitches. You're like my mother. She's all worried too."

I smile at the comparison to that beautiful blond woman I got to meet a few hours ago. "I'm going to take that as a compliment. I knew your mother would be pretty after seeing that picture of yours, but it didn't do her justice, Liam. She's absolutely beautiful. And your father? I can tell where you get your looks from. They're so sweet too! Your mother told me about how you loved marshmallows in your sweet potatoes when you were a little boy, so I made sure the kitchen has all the sweet potatoes and marshmallows you could possibly want."

His expression turns sheepish, and I swear I see a hint of guilt in his eyes. "What? What's wrong?" I ask, suddenly fearful I've upset him.

"I haven't eaten that since I was ten, Mia. I don't even like sweet potatoes anymore."

"It's okay. I hear they're healthy, so I'll make sure Ainsley and Mitchell know we have them in the house. I just won't mention the marshmallows so I don't have to hear a lecture from him about how much empty calories one marshmallow has in it."

I feel myself beginning to unravel after hearing

about my mistake with something he doesn't even like and hasn't eaten in over a decade. I only wanted to make sure he felt like he's at home as he's recuperating. That's all. He probably thinks I'm some stupid girl who just wants to buy everything in the world and bring it to my house because I'm feeling guilty that he got shot.

"Mia…"

He says my name in a low voice that sounds ominous. Like he's going to tell me he doesn't think he can go out on tour with me or he doesn't want to after getting shot because of what I did.

My entire body tenses up as I wait to hear the next words that come out of his mouth. He remains silent for so long, though, that I can't stop myself from filling the empty space with a bunch of chatter that means next to nothing.

"So, no sweet potatoes and marshmallows. I hope you told your mom so she doesn't make them for Thanksgiving or anything. I'm sure you will so she doesn't waste her time making something you don't like. There's a ton of other stuff down there, though, so don't worry. You can have whatever your heart desires. I have to admit I was surprised the media were waiting outside the hospital when we left. Can you believe those vultures? Someone gets shot, and all they want to do is take pictures. I'm sorry about that. I should have gone out a side door or something so they didn't swarm all over you."

Liam leans forward and holds out his hand toward where I sit on the bed. "Mia, come here."

Afraid of the serious tone of his voice and the somber expression he's wearing right now, I slide up the bed until I'm right next to him. He takes my hand in his, and for a moment, everything inside me calms, but then I look into his eyes and see that seriousness in them.

"Mia, you don't have to feel bad about what happened. I think that's what all of this is about, isn't it?"

I shake my head, refusing to admit the truth, especially to him. "No, not at all. I just need you to be in the best shape possible for when the tour starts in a few days. As for those goddamned reporters and photographers, that's how I always feel, but you didn't deserve to have to fight your way to the car after being in the hospital."

His warm skin against mine makes me feel like my insides are melting, but I don't see anything like that in him at all. I thought when we were out on that street that he was trying to tell me he cared but he didn't think he should. Did I misunderstand?

"I'm going to be fine. Honestly. It wasn't that bad. I guess I'm just a big bleeder, like the doctor said. And the press was nothing."

The mere mention of him bleeding out on that sidewalk as I hovered over him praying for anyone to stop him from dying brings tears to my eyes, and I hang my head so he can't see them. If I'm wrong and he didn't want to tell me he cares about me, the last thing I want is for him to see I'm that affected by him getting shot.

"Hey, what's wrong?"

I shake my head again, but it's no use. The tears come streaming down my cheeks like I'm some pathetic little girl who can't control her emotions.

"Mia, look at me."

When I refuse to do as he wants, he slides his finger under my chin and gently lifts it so he can see my tears. "I was so scared you'd die there, Liam. I didn't know what to do. I felt helpless, and I hate feeling that. I control everything in my life as much as I can, as you well know, but I couldn't do a thing to stop you from bleeding from that bullet."

"I do know you like to control everything and everyone, so I imagine seeing me down for the count was a lot to handle. I'm fine, though. See?"

He flexes his bicep to show me his right arm works fine, and I smile. "So you can show off? That doesn't mean you're fine. You got shot, Liam."

My teasing him makes him laugh. "Okay, I wasn't trying to show off, but you don't have to worry. It's going to be okay."

I hang my head and whisper the ugly truth I've hated since I saw him fall to the ground last night. "You got shot because of me. I don't know how I'll ever forgive myself for that."

With a heavy sigh, he says in that way that sounds so reasonable when I want to be completely unreasonable, "You didn't shoot me, so this isn't your fault. And I don't want to hear anything about how you left the estate and if I wasn't there, I wouldn't have been shot."

Smiling, I lift my head to see him smiling too. "Well, since you've taken away my entire argument for feeling guilty, I guess I can leave you feeling utterly innocent of my crime. Thank you, Liam."

"Go get ready for your first dates. You don't have much time, and there's no way I want to be the one your entourage blames when you aren't on fire that first night. And you know they will."

I can hear Ainsley and the rest of them already saying he's a distraction I shouldn't give into now that the tour is so close to beginning. Not that I give a damn what they have to say about Liam now. He took a bullet for me, and no matter how much he wants to claim I'm not to blame for him getting shot, the hard facts are if I hadn't dragged him down to that part of town and I hadn't run down that sidewalk making him chase me, he never would have been in any position to be shot by anyone.

"Thank you for not hating me, Liam."

The words barely come out loud enough for anyone but me to hear them, but when he nods and winks at me, I know he heard me. I don't know what I'd do if he hated me. Not after last night.

"If I didn't hate you when I first got here, there's no way I could hate you now. You saved me last night. Don't sell yourself short, Mia. You called 9-1-1 and told them exactly where to go. A lot of people would have unraveled, but you kept your cool. Things might have turned out way differently if you weren't there."

I know what he's trying to do, and even though I won't argue with him about it, he's wrong. I set everything into motion for him to get hurt last night. Whatever I did to help doesn't make up for what I did that made it possible for someone to shoot him.

Joking, I stand up from the bed and look down at him as I say, "Well, this hero needs to get working. Let me know if you need anything, okay?"

"I will. Go rehearse so you're ready for this weekend."

For a moment, our eyes lock and I think I'd like nothing more than to kiss him right now. I wonder if he's thinking that too.

CHAPTER FOUR

ia

HAPPY AFTER THE TIME I SPENT WITH LIAM, I practically bounce down the stairs and meet my mother and her assistant when I hit the first floor. She looks particularly dour today, but she's probably just worried about what happened last night. I get that. She never handles when I go out on my own, but the fact that someone got hurt is likely making her ten times as stressed out.

"I want to talk to you about your security situation, Mia," she says, frowning.

As much as I understand her concern, I'm not in the mood to discuss this. My security situation, as she calls it, is the best it's ever been. That's because of one person. Liam. Now that I know he's going to be fine and right there with me when I go out on tour, I have nothing to worry about.

"Later," I say, pushing her off like I will every time she brings this up.

"No, now. With Liam laid up, we need to address your security. I think we should bring Michael back."

I stop, stunned by her suggestion. Spinning around, I try to make out if she's serious or not. "You want to bring Michael back? Why? I don't need anyone new, or in this case, old."

Setting her jaw like she always does when she insists on something, my mother takes a step toward me. "Liam is upstairs in his bed, which is perfectly natural since he's been shot. That said, he's not in any shape to protect you, and you need someone by your side when the first shows begin this weekend. We've got the media camped out on the street because they sense a story here. If ever you needed security, it's now. It's too late to get anyone else to replace Liam, so Michael's the logical answer to the problem."

My brain spins at the fact that she's serious about this. "There is no problem, first of all, so I don't need a solution. Liam is resting, as the doctor said he has to, but he'll be by my side when the tour starts. The first few dates are right here in Tampa, and all of his guys he's brought in to assist him can help him if he needs it, which he won't. It's just a few stitches in his upper arm. This isn't some injury he received on the battlefield. He'll be fine, so thanks but no thanks about Michael."

Still, she doesn't back down, even after I've told

her no to replacing Liam. And why is she acting like having the media obsessed with me isn't exactly what she works to cultivate with every move she makes?

"Mia, I handle security for you, and I'm the one who brought Liam in, if you remember. Let me handle things. It's only until he's back up on his feet. We don't really have a choice. Michael is the only one who can come with such short notice."

Everything she says confuses me. Shaking my head in disbelief, I struggle to understand why she's being like this.

"You were the one who fired Michael for helping me get that hotel room and sneaking me out. Now you think he's the only person in the world who can pick up whatever slack you're sure is going to happen now since Liam's been shot? Not the guys he trusts and handpicked to work with him to protect me because he wanted to shore up my security, which by the way was so lax that I probably was in more danger than anyone wants to talk about? No! Let Michael stay with his hoochie mama at his apartment. That's where he belongs."

Before she can try to give me another reason why I should take that poor excuse for a bodyguard back, I hurry over to Ainsley's room to talk out all these things I'm feeling about Liam. I know she isn't crazy about him, but that's good because she'll be happy to give me all the Devil's advocate arguments she can think of.

When she opens her door, I march right in, ready to talk about everything that's going on with Liam and me. Ainsley looks a little surprised but doesn't complain about my not asking to come in. Maybe she thinks after what I went through last night that she shouldn't give me a hard time.

"We need to talk," I announce as I flop down in the weird saggy chair with the blue cushions over near the window.

"Okay," she says warily. "What about?"

"I need you to be as tough on me as I need, but remember that my feelings are a little all over the place today, okay?"

Ainsley sits down on her bed and crosses her legs under her. "Okay. I thought for a second there that you had some problem with me, but now I'm confused. What do I have to be tough on you about? Hey, shouldn't you be rehearsing with Tiffany and your dancers? The tour begins in only a few days."

"That's not what I need you to be tough on me about, but thanks. I'll get to her and them in a few minutes. First, though, I need you to give me all the reasons why I shouldn't care about Liam."

My life coach levels her harsh gaze directly on my face and grimaces. "You sure you want me to go there? Because there are about a million small reasons and one big reason I can give you for not falling for him."

I shrug, hopeful when she hears the truth that I'm already crazy about him that she won't pitch a fit. "Too late. I've already fallen."

"Then what the hell is this conversation for?" she asks in exasperation.

"To help me figure out what to do! Stop being so difficult. The man protected me last night after someone shot him. You act as if he's some scum off the street."

She lets out a heavy sigh full of irritation. "Fine. He did his job. Yay for him. That's no reason to fall head over heels in love with him."

My face heats up from a blush at her mention of love. "I didn't say I was head over heels in love with him. God, you are such a drama queen. I said I've fallen for him. Not in love. Let's just say in caring for him."

"Fall in care with someone? Okay, so now we're just making shit up? At least I know the rules of this conversation. So you care for him? Why? That seems like a good place to start. Tell me why you care for Mr. Rules and Regulations, who by the way hates your dear friend, yours truly."

"He doesn't hate you. He just hates how you sound like you're giving birth to goats when you do your evening stretches," I say, struggling to hold back my laughter.

But Ainsley doesn't find any of it funny.

"He's crazy uptight. Like if you stuck coal up his ass, you'd be able to pull out a diamond in a week."

I scrunch up my face at that visual. "I'm not sure if you're trying to make me dislike him or you with that description, Ains. Can we get back to talking about my caring for him? I need you to tell me why I shouldn't."

"Because he's your chief of security. That sounds like a good place to start. Isn't he breaking some kind of personal code of ethics people like him make a pledge to uphold when they take a job?" she asks in a tone that tells me she thinks he is.

"I don't know. Is that really a thing?" I ask, wondering if Liam could get into trouble for caring for me.

That isn't what I want. Nobody should be able to dictate who falls for who, especially if it means he might get in trouble with the owner of VIP over it.

"It should be," Ainsley says in a huff. "You still haven't answered my question. Why do you think you care for him?"

That's easier asked than answered. There are a hundred reasons why I care about Liam. He's good looking. I could tell Ainsley that, but since she thinks he's way too uptight, it probably wouldn't be an answer she'll agree with.

He's great at his job. That's a good reason, especially since his job revolves around protecting my life. Then again, she'll probably just say he's supposed to be good at his job.

He makes me smile. I like listening to him talk about his family and the nature shows he likes just as I do. I feel comfortable whenever I'm with him.

"Well? I think if you can't answer the question of why you care about him, then that's your answer why you shouldn't."

God, she is in rare, militant form today. Is this what everyone means when they say tough love?

Taking a deep breath in, I let it out slowly and tell her why I care for him. "Because when I'm around him, I'm happier than when I'm not around him."

Her eyes open wide, and I suspect she thinks that's the biggest load of shit she's ever heard. It's the truth, though. Even last night when I was trying to run away, simply having him with me made me feel better. I didn't really want him to leave me alone. I just didn't know how to handle all the emotions rushing through me after what happened between us.

And then as soon as I saw him bleeding from a bullet that may have been meant for me, I realized how much I'd miss him if he wasn't in my life.

My life coach's body looks like it deflates at my answer. "Well, I wasn't expecting something so deep. I thought you were going to mention his beautiful body or how he looks when he's working out in the gym. I'm impressed, Mia."

With a shrug, I smile. "Don't be. I like those things too, so let's not get me set up for sainthood just yet. But other than abs that make my mouth water and how incredible he looks when he wears those gray sweatpants of his, I really like spending time with him."

I don't tell her the hundred other things I like about Liam, but even with what I've said, I know I'm in trouble. Ainsley knows it too. I see it in her expression as she tries to smile at me.

"You're not helping with arguments against him, Ains. Where did they go?"

Her cheeks blush a deep pink and she giggles. "With those gray sweatpants. Nothing I can say to you can beat gray sweatpants. Those are kryptonite to women. Why do you think guys wear them?"

We both laugh, but she's right. A hot man in gray sweatpants is truly the one thing that can make a woman forget everything she was thinking at that moment.

I stand up to leave, not any clearer on what I'm going to do about Liam. "Well, this wasn't helpful at all, but something tells me nothing was going to be anyway."

"I'm sorry. I'm really not a huge fan of his, but it's hard to have an argument against someone making you happy. What are you going to do? I mean, does he know how you feel? Have you said anything to him yet?"

Shaking my head, I admit the sad truth. "No, and I don't know how to do that. I thought last night when we were downtown that he was trying to say he cared for me, but now I'm not so sure. This whole getting shot thing has totally made things so much worse but a lot better too."

Ainsley looks at me in horror, so I quickly explain what I mean. "Not that I ever wanted him to get shot. It's not like that, so stop looking at me like I'm some kind of terrible person. It's just that it's given us a chance to just be nice to one another, which I really like. I don't mind sparring with him since even when he's fighting with me, I know he's only trying to help, but simply sitting next to him as he lies in bed is nice too."

I bury my face in my hands. "Oh, God, I don't know what I'm going to do."

She hurries over to me and takes me in her arms. "Don't worry so much. You have a lot on your plate right now. Take a deep breath, remember your priorities, and above all, don't freak out. Everything will work out for the best. It always does."

As I inhale and exhale, trying to calm myself like she claims I should, thoughts of my mother trying to push Liam out to bring Michael back flood my brain. I can't believe she thinks that's going to ever happen.

"You don't feel like you're relaxing, Mia."

I drop my hands from my face and explain why. "My mother wants to replace Liam with Michael until he's better. I told her no and put my foot down, but something tells me she's planning on doing it anyway. What the hell is she thinking? She's acting like Liam is bedridden or something. He just needs to rest for a day or so. God, my life is a mess, and I have to go out on tour in just a couple days."

My life coach pats my arm like she's afraid I'm going to completely unravel right there in her room if she doesn't pull her social worker thing on me. "Calm down. Seriously, I need you to relax. Whatever happens, you can handle it. I'll be right there beside you the entire time, so deep breaths. Do you want me to talk to Andrea? I can let her know this kind of stress isn't good for you right before a tour. That might make her back off a little."

The last thing I need is my best friend and my mother brawling over how much stress I have in my life, so I shake my head and smile. "No, but thanks. I hope she got the idea that I wasn't having any of that Michael coming back nonsense, but if she brings it up again, I'll have to handle it. As you always tell me, the key to being happy is to know when to ignore the bullshit. So I'll ignore it and her, if she keeps it up."

As I walk toward her door to leave, she chuckles. "I do say that. It just sounds a lot more strident coming from you. Maybe try smiling when you say it?"

Looking back at her, I paste a grin on my face. "Ignoring the bullshit is the key to being happy. Any better?"

"No, still pretty harsh."

"Oh, well."

Maybe harsh is what I have to be to get things the way I want when it comes to my mother.

ia

ALL OF US SIT AROUND IN MY DRESSING ROOM AS always to do our preshow ritual I've done since the first time I went out on tour. Back then, it was a tiny event that consisted of malls and galleries that held no more than a couple hundred people. Still, it was exciting in those days since I was only fifteen and couldn't do bars and clubs like other performers just starting out. But whether it's a mall show or one in front of an arena full of screaming fans, my entourage and I always sit together and share good vibes we want to carry us through that night's performance.

"Okay, everyone! Time to join hands," Ainsley announces to the entire group. "It's almost time for Mia to go out and see her fans, and we want to send her off with the best possible feeling we can."

One by one, each person I rely on to make me look beautiful and toned and talented, along with my five dancers for the night, steps up into the center of the rather small dressing room at the Citrus County Pavilion. We all take the hand of the person next to us and close our eyes as I try to channel all the gratitude and happiness I have inside me.

"Thank you for all these incredible people who make my professional and personal life so much better than I ever dreamed possible. Let us have a great show and give my fans what they came here tonight to see."

As usual and our tradition, Mitchell chimes in with his lame joke, "Okay, break a leg! Well, not really because working out with a broken leg is complete crap and I don't want to have to deal with that."

By the time he finishes, everyone's eyes are open and we're all staring at my trainer in amused disbelief that he thinks any of that is funny. He's a terrific guy, but his sense of humor is shit.

"Thanks, Mitch. And thank you everyone! Let's have a great show tonight!"

Everyone cheers and throws their hands up in the air. This feels good, and I'm looking forward to the start of a fantastic tour with this show. We're all happy and rested, and I've got the best security man in the world protecting me.

What else could a girl like me ask for?

As everyone files out of the dressing room to leave me alone for the last few minutes before show time, I wonder where Liam has been for the past hour. I've seen each of his men milling around, but he's been absent.

Probably double and triple checking everything. He does like to be thorough. I like that about him.

A member of the stage crew opens the dressing room door just enough to fit his lips into the space. "Sorry if I'm barging in on you, Mia, but fifteen minutes until show time."

He closes the door before I get a chance to thank him. Fifteen minutes. Like always, this is when I start to get nervous. I look down at my hand resting on my dressing table and it's trembling. I have nothing to be scared about. Liam and his men have taken care of security and made it tighter than it ever was.

For a few seconds, my mind races with the thought that the bullet that hit Liam wasn't meant for him but for me. Is it possible my stalker has taken things up a notch and turned to attempted murderer?

I shake my head in disbelief. No way. For all this time, he's only been a stalker and now suddenly, he's taken to trying to kill me? That doesn't make sense.

But if the shooter wasn't him, who was it? Of course, the police say they have nothing yet. It feels like every time something happens with me, that's all they have to tell me. "Nothing yet, Mia. We're working on finding all the clues we can and solving this, but it will take time."

Time my ass. I doubt they'll ever figure out who took that shot at Liam and me. Then again, maybe because it involved another person, the cops will actually try to solve this crime.

A knock on the dressing room door tears me out of my miserable thoughts about the police, and I hope to see Liam walking in to tell me he's checked everything and it's all as safe as can be. Then I'll get back to dealing with the preshow jitters that always plague me on first nights.

But when my mother walks through the door instead of him, I'm disappointed and don't bother pretending I'm not. "What do you want, Mother? I'm busy trying to get myself into the right mindset right now, so whatever you want to talk about, it can wait."

She forces a smile in response to my coldness and hurries over to where I sit. "I love that costume! I didn't realize you were returning to your red look for this show. You always look so great when you wear red on stage, Mia."

Her compliments make me smile, but I sense something frantic about her as she practically trips over her words. "Thanks, Mom. The girls and I talked it over and we decided red felt right for this tour. I want people to be wowed, and even though *Mine* has hit the top of the charts before the whole record releases, I feel like I have something to prove with this tour."

That's the most I've talked about my music and my songs to my mother in months. I didn't mean to confess all of that to her, especially since she rarely enjoys hearing about the artistic side of the business. She's all about the money side, and I have a feeling if it were up to her, she'd have me singing the same song over and over on a constant loop if it made money.

My talk about how this tour feels for me surprises her, but she nods like she understands, or at least like she wants me to think she understands. "Of course, the song is doing well. The entire record will too. Your millions and millions of fans love you, Mia. It's why this show tonight is packed, even though it's just a warm-up show to work out all the kinks."

"The audience doesn't think of this show that way," I say, reflexively wanting to defend my fans.

They don't view early dates on my tours like practice sessions, and they shouldn't. I would never want these fans tonight to think they got a lesser version of me or my performance simply because they showed up for the first date. These are my hometown fans, people who have watched me grow up from that little girl at the malls singing her heart out for a couple hundred people. They were there before the rest of the world. They deserve nothing but my best for being my fans the longest.

"Yes, yes," she says, not truly agreeing with me but placating me as she fixes the strap of my costume on my left shoulder.

God, I hate when she does that. I'm a grown woman, but as soon as I sense my mother placating me about anything, I turn into a pre-adolescent girl who wants to do nothing more than stomp her feet and have a temper tantrum.

"What did you come in for anyway?" I ask, tired of this dance the two of us do.

Suddenly, she looks guilty, like I caught her in the middle of doing something wrong. Looking away toward the sofa on the other side of the room, she says, "I just wanted to check that you were ready."

"This isn't my first rodeo, you know. I know I need to be ready, especially since Carl popped his head in a few minutes ago to say it was fifteen minutes until show time."

"Good, good. Well, I'll get out of your hair then. I just wanted to make sure you'll be ready when security comes to take you out to the stage," she says with her back toward me as she walks toward the door.

"I'll be ready. In fact, please send Liam in now so I can talk to him before I have to go out there."

My mother stops just as her hand lands on the doorknob, but she doesn't say anything for a long moment, further irritating me. Why does she have to be so dramatic about everything? All she needs to do is say okay and then walk out. Why act like this is some scene in a damn movie?

Slowly, she turns around and gives me the fakest smile I've ever seen on her face. Even faker than the ones she used to put on when I acted up and everyone thought she was to blame since I was underage.

The type of smile that means she's hiding something.

"About that."

"About what? Just send Liam in and stop making this whole thing a melodrama with you as the lead actress, okay? I need to get prepared to go out on stage in less than ten minutes."

"He's not here."

I've never been diagnosed with high blood pressure, but I swear at this moment I feel like the top of my head is about to blow off, spraying blood and brains all over this goddamned room. A headache instantly begins to throb at my temples, and my face feels like it's suddenly ten degrees hotter than the rest of my body.

When I stand up, I can barely keep myself from falling over. "What do you mean he's not here?"

"He wasn't ready to protect you for tonight's show. I knew it the second I saw him having one of his guys help him with that sling he has to wear. So tonight and tomorrow night, Michael will be your personal bodyguard and take you to the stage."

"What the hell did you do?" I say, feeling the tears start to well in my eyes as I struggle to keep my emotions in check. "The first night of the tour and you pull this shit?"

She moves into hyperplacate mode like she always has when she's fucked up and I dare to tell her I won't stand for it. "Now don't get upset, Mia. It's only for a couple of shows. You should have seen him. He just can't do the job like I know he wants to, so I told him I'd have someone else do it so he could rest. Liam knows his men are right here for you. That's why he was perfectly fine with it."

I can't control my emotions anymore and scream, "Get out! Get out now! Leave me alone!"

My outburst startles her and she quickly hurries out of the room like some guilty thing who knows if she doesn't get the hell out of my sight at this very moment that she risks me really blowing up on her. I collapse back down onto the chair and look around for some explanation how this could have happened after I explicitly told her I didn't want her to replace Liam with Michael.

Oh, God. Liam isn't here. I can't do this knowing he's miles away back at the house. How could he just let me come here without being by my side?

CHAPTER SIX

*M*ia

QUICKLY, I SCRAMBLE TO FIND MY CELL PHONE. I need to talk to him. I need to understand how he could let her do this. He knows how much I rely on him to be around me to feel safe.

He answers with his usual hello that sounds so casual that I want to scream. How can he be so calm at a moment like this? After all his lectures on how important my security should be to me and how it used to be practically Swiss cheese with all the holes in what Michael used to do for me, the first time I truly expected to have him in charge and he's back at the estate in bed watching some nature show?

"Liam, why aren't you here?" I ask, practically sobbing.

"Mia, what's wrong? Aren't you supposed to be going on in like three minutes?"

"Why aren't you here? My mother told me she replaced you. You're okay with that? Tonight, of all nights, you're okay with me being with lame security?"

"You don't have lame security," he says and then chuckles like any of this is fucking funny. "My guys are there, so trust me, there's nothing lame about your protection. Trust me."

I stand up to pace as the realization that my mother lied to him about everything concerning this show tonight. My legs feel like they're going to give out, but I can't sit down because I swear I'm going to explode at any moment.

"Your guys aren't handling my security tonight. My mother brought Michael back to replace you. She told me she wanted to do that the other day, but I flatly refused to agree to it. She knew I needed you here tonight, and still she went behind my back and brought Michael back. He's the one in charge, not your guys, Liam."

"What? That's impossible. Drew's supposed to be in charge, Mia. I made sure of that before they left here today. Your mother knew that too since I talked to her this afternoon. Why didn't she tell me she was planning to bring in someone new? He doesn't know any of the plans."

"He's not new! He's Michael, the one you told me was the shittiest bodyguard you'd ever heard of. He's the one in charge, and I swear to God I won't leave this room if she sends him down here to walk me to the stage. I won't."

My emotions are spiraling out of control so much that I don't think even Ainsley and her Zen stuff could calm me down now. My mother has done some terrible things in her time, but this is the worst. She knows I've been on edge since Liam got shot, and she turns around and brings Michael back after she fired him for being such a terrible security chief? What the hell is wrong with her?

"Listen to me, Mia. I want you to relax. This is all under control. I'll call Drew and find out what's going on. Give me a couple minutes and then I'll call you back. Don't worry. My guys wouldn't let me down and they won't let you down either."

When I don't say anything, he adds, "Trust me. I'll handle this and then you won't have to worry about any of it. You'll just be able to have a great show and thrill all those fans who are dying to see you, okay? I saw on the news that the line of people to get in is the biggest the Pavilion has ever had."

"Okay. Just fix this, Liam. I don't want to have him in charge. I don't feel safe without you."

"I will. I'll call you right back."

Slamming my phone down onto the table, I consider storming out to find my mother and firing her insubordinate ass for doing this on the biggest night I've had in so long. She knows how important these first shows are to me and everyone else in the crew. This is where we get the feel for how things are and what needs to be tweaked a little so everything runs smoothly when we're out on the road miles away from home. How could she pull this on me tonight?

A knock on the dressing room door startles me, and the next thing I know, there is Michael smiling at me like we're the best of friends and he didn't treat me like I never meant a thing to him the second my traitorous mother fired him just six weeks ago. His expression comes off as smug, like he always knew he'd get his job back and nothing he did to me would matter.

Well, he's wrong. Now he'll get to find out just how mistaken he was.

"Don't say a word because I don't want to hear a thing from you. Just turn around and walk out the way you came in. You are not my bodyguard anymore, so you don't belong in here. Whatever my mother told you was wrong, so leave."

Michael runs his hand through his dark hair and smiles. "Good to know some things don't change. I was wondering if you'd settled down since I left. I see you haven't."

"This isn't some happy reunion, Michael. This is me telling you to get the fuck out or I swear to God I'm going to scream at the top of my lungs until the cops haul your ass away from here," I snap, hating the very sight of this man.

My phone begins to vibrate across the table, so I quickly grab it and see it's Liam. The second I put the phone to my ear, I hear him say to me, "Mia, I just talked to Drew. I don't know what your mother is up to, but she's all but cut my guys out tonight. All they've been told is Michael is in charge, but when they've tried to brief him on the plans I set up, he walks away. I'm getting ready to leave right now. I'll be there as soon as I can."

Before I can say a word, the call ends. Furious at the man standing in front of me and my mother, I spin around to face Michael and shake my head. Whatever the two of them thought was going to happen tonight isn't, thanks to Liam.

"You and my mother screwed up, pal. You think you can just upend everything because she wants you back? Fuck you! I don't want you back, and my new chief of security is pissed that you've made a mess of his plans to protect me. So get the hell out and go tell my mother than I'm not leaving this dressing room until Liam gets here, so she better goddamned hope there isn't a lot of traffic or this fucking show won't happen at all."

My former bodyguard takes a step back and shakes his head. "Still doing the diva act, Mia? Fine. I'll tell her, but everyone's going to hate you for doing this just because you can't have your way."

"I'm doing this because I don't feel safe without the one person who makes me feel fucking safe, you asshole!" I scream. "Tell my mother that too!"

When he leaves, I sit down again, weak from too much yelling and knowing I've probably wrecked my voice for tonight. I can't decide if I want to cry or hit something. Or both.

My mother knows someone shot Liam not ten feet away from where I was standing, and she feels like bringing in some guy who made me feel like shit after she fired him is the logical next step she should take? I don't think I'm ever going to forgive her for this.

How can I?

I hear the crowd cheering for me to come out and entertain them like I'm supposed to. I want to. They have no idea how much I want to be out there singing my heart out for them on every goddamned song.

But I can't do it if I don't feel safe, and without Liam, I can't leave this room. I won't.

The door flies open, and my mother storms in like she's got a bone to pick with me. She's as mistaken as her idiot new best friend if she thinks I'm going to just sit here and take her nonsense now.

"Michael says you won't come out. Is that true?" she asks in some kind of fake shocked voice.

"Your little errand boy moves quickly when he wants to. What did you promise you'd give him to get him to behave so well, Mother?" I ask, staring into her dark eyes to find the truth of her feelings.

"Don't be ridiculous. You're making a fool of yourself, Mia. Michael is doing us a favor, one he didn't have to agree to after I fired him and you made that scene at his apartment. Now let's get going because your adoring fans are waiting."

She turns toward the door as if her simply saying I have to go is all it takes. My feet feel like they're encased in cement, though. I'm not leaving this room without seeing Liam and knowing he's got everything under control.

"No. When Liam gets here, then I'll go because I'll

know I'll be safe. So you and Michael go find yourselves someplace to bitch about me until then because I'm not budging from this room."

My mother's eyes open wide, and I know she isn't pretending to be shocked now. I've been stubborn on a great many points in the past with her, but I've never sounded like I do tonight.

"The press is going to cut you to shreds for this little stunt, Mia. Maybe you should think about that."

I open my mouth to say maybe I'll mention just who the architect of tonight's mess is, but she leaves before I can get a word out. Staring at the gray metal door as she slams it shut, I swear to myself that I'd fire her if she wasn't my mother.

Maybe I will fire her even though she is.

CHAPTER SEVEN

iam

SYLVESTER MAY DO HIS JOB AT THE ESTATE FRONT gate well, but as a driver in a dire situation, the guy sucks. A mile away from the Citrus County Pavilion and twenty minutes after Mia was supposed to start her show, he and I are stuck in a traffic jam that hasn't moved an inch in five minutes.

"Fuck! What's the goddamned hold up?" I grumble as I crane my neck to see why the hell we're all sitting here on a four lane highway.

"I think these are all of Mia's fans," he says in guilty voice, as if he told all of these people to basically make the road a parking lot.

"Sorry, man. I'm just frustrated and worried what's going to happen if I don't get to this show in the next few minutes."

He gives me a tepid smile I hope means he's accepted my apology, and I stick my head out the passenger side window in an attempt to figure out what the major malfunction is all around us. But he's right. It's Mia's fans all going to the show, so this bottleneck isn't going to get cleared anytime soon.

I have no choice. I have to get to her and clean up the mess her mother made with this Michael rehiring.

"Okay, Sylvester, I think this is where I get off. I'm sorry you're going to be trapped here for a while, but I'm hoofing it from here on out."

As I open the door, he gives me a shocked look like he can't believe what I just said and mumbles, "Okay. Are you planning on walking the mile to the pavilion?"

With a chuckle, I nod before stepping out of the car. "Something like that. Take care. I'll see you back at the house. Wish me luck!"

I slam the door shut and take off down the highway, weaving between cars as they slowly inch toward my destination. A few people holler at me, cheering me on as they watch me run past their cars like this is some kind of publicity stunt.

They have no idea. I have a feeling if I don't get to Mia and fix what her mother fucked up, watching me run through traffic is going to be the most fun many of these people have tonight.

It doesn't take me long to reach the pavilion, my right arm in a sling and all, but even though I work out every day, I'm winded after sprinting that mile. I'm more of a distance runner, if anything, but desperate times call for desperate measures.

The first person I see who I recognize is Kip, and I instantly know things are much worse than I imagined on my way here. His usually calm façade is nowhere to be found, replaced by a look of pure worry.

His eyes light up when he sees me, though. "Jesus Christ, Liam. You look like you ran all the way here, man. I thought you were supposed to stay in bed to rest for a couple days."

I take a deep breath in an attempt to get my heart back to some semblance of a normal beat and shake my head. "I'll rest when I'm dead. Right now, I've got other things to worry about. What the fuck is going on? I got a call from Mia saying her mother brought in the old head of security. Then Drew told me he cut you guys out. Where can I go to watch her from the side of the stage so I can make sure everything's okay?"

"She never went on. The crowd is ready to explode, and she's nowhere to be found. I heard her mother complaining that she refuses to perform. I'm telling you, Liam, somebody better get out on that stage and start singing or these people are going to freak."

The sound of thousands of people cheering for Mia all around me says Kip's right. "Let me see if I can do something about that. Gather up all our guys and meet me at the dressing room. Our plan we put in place when we did the walkthrough the other day is still the one that's in effect. Fuck that Michael guy. He must think we're goddamned rookies."

I don't usually let my crew see me react to anything

with emotion, but this pisses me off. Andrea knew we had everything in order. What the hell was she thinking when she brought that guy back into the mix?

"Okay! Now you're talking! Let's just hope the crowd doesn't decide to storm the place before you get everything settled."

Nodding, I silently pray for the same thing as I turn to head back to the dressing room. Local officials and security line the passageway, but I hurry past them to get to the one person I know needs to see me.

The dressing room door is closed, and when I try the doorknob, I find it locked. Quickly, I knock a few times and say loud enough for anyone to hear, "Mia, it's Liam! Let me in!"

A second later, the door flies open and I see Mia and her entire entourage and all her dancers staring at me. Mia runs to me and throws her arms around my body, clinging to me like I'm all that's keeping her safe right now.

"Liam! Everything is a disaster. I can't do this. My mother made everything a mess."

I look down at her sobbing against me and know things are much worse than I anticipated. I need to get her calm, but before I can do that, I need to get all these people out of this dressing room.

"Don't worry. We'll fix this and you'll be singing for all those people tonight."

I march in and immediately begin directing everyone out to where they belong. Pointing toward the door, I focus on the dancers first. "This show is about to start, so go take your places and be ready when Mia needs you."

The five women dutifully hurry out into the hallway, so I turn my attention to all the people who live at the house with us. "I need to speak to Mia, so everyone out. This chaos needs to end right now, so if you want to help her, find my security guys outside the door and they'll tell you where to safely position yourselves. That crowd is nearly at a fever pitch, and I don't want any of you getting hurt because you're in the wrong spot."

I expect to get some resistance from at least one or two of them, especially that life coach, but they all hurry out like the dancers did a few seconds ago, and finally, I'm alone with Mia. She still holds on to me like I'm a life raft, so I gently pry her arms from around my waist and smile down at her.

"Things are way more exciting than I expected them to be," I say with a chuckle. "You didn't tell me it would be pandemonium."

Her dark eyes stare up at me, and I can see beyond all the stage makeup that she's been crying. "My mother must have lost her mind. How could she do this to me on my first night of the tour?"

That's the question I want to have answered, but for now, I've got more important things to tackle. Taking Mia by the hand, I guide her over to the sofa and sit down next to her. I don't know anything about calming a performer before a big show, but I know this woman well enough to understand she needs to think of something good right now or she's never going to be able to walk out onto that stage.

"I left poor Sylvester out on the highway that looks like a parking lot because all of your fans are trying to get here. I guess it's a good thing for those people that things are running behind, huh?"

Mia hangs her head and sighs. "I bet you think I'm some spoiled rotten diva who's misbehaving, don't you?"

I shake my head and smile. "Nope. Not this time. This time, I'm putting all the blame on your mother. But we can't fix that right now. I need to get you out in front of all those people who can't wait to see you."

She looks up at me and smiles, and then her eyes get big. "Did you have to run down the highway to get here? You did that for me?"

Nodding, I shrug, happy to minimize my mile long sprint at this moment. "It's my job. You told me you needed me, so here I am. That's what a bodyguard does for the person he's guarding."

"I can't believe you did that for me. Nobody's ever done anything like that for me when I asked them for help."

"Well, now I need you to do something for me, okay?"

Mia narrows her eyes, like she isn't sure what I could need at this moment. "What's that?"

Silent for a few moments, I let the noise of the crowd waiting for her fill the room. "Hear that? Those are the people who want nothing more than to see you perform, so I need you to forget all about your mother and her nonsense and go out there to give those people what only you can give them. Nobody else in the world is going to make them happier than you can just by singing your songs, Mia."

An expression of fear washes over her. "I don't know if I can, Liam. I feel so emotional right now. Even worse, I've been screaming at my mother for the past half hour, so I can only imagine what I'm going to sound like when I try to hit that first high note."

I take her hand in mine and give it a tiny squeeze. "You can because this is what you're great at. Everything else is bullshit we can deal with later. Right now, you need to go show that crowd what you can do. I know you can do this."

For a long moment, I'm not sure Mia believes she can do it, though, but she takes a deep breath in and smiles, nodding like she wants to try. "Okay. Thank you, Liam. I don't know what I'd do without you."

The fact that her mother wanted to see exactly what Mia would do without me tonight is what I plan to find out as soon as I locate Andrea. In the meantime, at least I've made the one person who needed to know she's safe feel like she can do this tonight.

She stands up and turns to look at me. "You'll be on the side of the stage, right? I don't think I can do this without knowing you're nearby so everything's safe."

I stand up and smile. "I'll be there, along with all of my men just where they're supposed to be."

Like she did when she saw me when I first arrived

here, she throws her arms around my waist and presses her cheek to my chest. Her body trembles next to mine, and even though I know I shouldn't hug her back, it's like I can't stop myself. She's so frail right now that I can't let her think I'm not here for her in any way she needs.

The truth is that I like how she feels against me. Far too much, in fact. Alarms go off in my head as we stand there in each other's arms, but I ignore them by telling myself that it would be cruel to push her away at the very moment she needs to believe she has someone who cares about her.

That's a lie, though, and no matter how I try to convince myself I'm being some selfless guy to help her perform tonight, the truth is I care far too much about Mia to want to see her unhappy like she was earlier.

"Liam, I couldn't do this without you. I hope you know that," she says against me.

I don't respond, afraid anything I say will make her realize how much I know I shouldn't be standing here with her like this. Instead, I softly slide my hand up and down her back, as if that's any less a violation of all the rules I've always followed in my job. Her red satin dress feels so cool under my palm that I let myself get lost in the sensation for a moment, but thankfully, a knock on the dressing room door puts an end to my fantasizing.

Gently, I push her away and hold her by the shoulders as I look deep into her eyes. "Okay, I'm guessing that's one of my guys saying that if I don't get you out there that people will be coming after us with torches and pitchforks, so what do you say you go show them why they've waited this long?"

Mia takes another deep breath and lets it out in a rush as she nods her agreement. "Okay. Let's do this!"

When I take a step toward the door to leave before her, she stops me with a touch to my arm. I look back, and in a flash, she's up on her toes softly giving me a kiss I don't think I'll ever forget.

She pulls away, and with a sexy grin, she says, "Now I'm ready."

Jesus, I don't think I'm strong enough to not want this woman. Not when she does things like that and makes my legs weak.

I open the door and see my crew waiting for us. Kip and Jack know that's their cue to take their positions near the front of the stage while the rest of us escort Mia to the back of the stage.

The cheers of the crowd grow louder and louder until I'm not sure I can hear a thing anyone says to me as we make our way through the long passageway. Right before we reach the stairs that go up to the stage, I see Andrea. Mia reaches back right behind her to search for my hand, and I quickly grasp it to let her know nobody, not even her mother, can hurt her now that I'm there.

As we pass her, I mouth, "You and I will be talking about what happened when this is all over."

Andrea may not be able to hear me, but she understands what I'm saying and the angry look on my face as a warning that she better not pull any more bullshit tonight. I don't know what her plans were with Michael, but I intend on finding out. If she was innocently trying to help protect her daughter, then fine.

If she wasn't, then we're going to have to talk, and she's not going to like what I have to say.

With each step I climb behind Mia toward the stage, my heart races more and more. I've guarded important people before, but never in my life have I heard so many people yelling and cheering for anyone I'm protecting. My instinct makes me want to whisk her away from here so she can be safe and not have to hear all this deafening noise, but I have to fight that because I know this is where she belongs.

And if I didn't, the moment we reach the stage and she turns around to smile at me, I'd know then. Before my eyes, Mia blossoms into someone bigger than life. She's more beautiful and more desirable than she's ever been since the day I met her, and I know right then why millions of people adore her.

I can't hear a thing above the sound of the crowd, but I watch her as she mouths back to me, "Thank you."

A second later, she lets go of my hand and steps out onto that stage, and thousands of people go wild. For a few moments, I can't move I'm so mesmerized by this woman, but then the show starts and I know I have to switch into work mode.

I search the sides of the stage to make sure everyone's in their assigned place and see my men have this handled. Michael lurks near the very back of the stage like some thief who can't wait to get away, but he's nothing now.

Mia opens her arms wide and makes a motion like she's hugging the entire audience before she says, "Thank you for waiting for me! I love you! Thank you!"

The crowd goes even wilder than before, and she sweetly giggles as she offers an explanation for why she's over thirty minutes late. "I'm sorry it took me so long to get here to you. At the last minute, my strap on my dress snapped, and I know you wouldn't want me to have a wardrobe malfunction right here in front of all of you."

Cheers and cries of "We love you, Mia" fill the air around us, and she blows them all kisses. "But now I'm here and ready to give you my best. Are you ready?"

I watch in awe as she makes them forget with a few simple words that they waited all that time for her, charming them before she even sings a single note. She really does belong out there with them. It's like I'm seeing a completely different person than I have all these weeks at the estate.

And I have to admit, I'm crazy about this Mia.

Then, when I don't think I can admire her more, she looks back at me and smiles before turning to face the audience. "I want to begin with a song that means the world to me, even more now because I can honestly say I know what it feels to be truly cared for. This is to the one person who makes me feel safer than I've ever known was possible."

I hear her begin to sing the first words of her hit song *Always There* and realize she's singing it about me. Out of the corner of my eye, I see Drew raise his eyebrows to let me know he knows too.

At that moment, I know one thing for sure. I'm in trouble because I'm crazy about this woman.

There's only one problem.

I'm not supposed to be. It breaks every rule a bodyguard follows. It breaks every rule I've lived my professional life by all these years and through all the jobs I've taken.

And I don't care.

ia

I FEEL LIKE I'M FLOATING ON CLOUD NINE BY THE time the night ends. When I settle in with the crew to celebrate a fantastic first night show, I can't help but feel Liam and his men belong right here down at the pool with us. They made it possible for me to perform and feel this incredible.

Well, Liam made it possible. Not that his guys didn't help, but if it wasn't for him rushing over to the pavilion to take care of the mess my mother made, I never would have been able to walk out onto that stage.

Ainsley hands me a glass of champagne and raises hers in the air. "To Mia! Congratulations, girl! Tonight was unbelievable. I don't think I've ever seen you perform like that. It was like you were a different person."

She's right. I felt different tonight. I felt loved and protected like never before, and it came through loud and clear in every word I sang.

Everyone raises their glass to toast me and my performance, making me feel like the queen of the world. "To Mia!"

As they all begin to talk amongst themselves, Ainsley pulls me aside and whispers, "I have to know what happened when you and Liam were alone in your dressing room for all that time."

I roll my eyes at the less-than-subtle suggestion I see in her expression as she wiggles her eyebrows. "Not that."

Faking innocence, she shakes her head and opens her eyes wide like she can't believe I could think she was suggesting he and I had sex in the dressing room. "What? It might have happened. You never know. Since you were so happy, I was just wondering."

"I was happy because I knew I was safe when Liam showed up to take over security. Once I knew he was in charge again instead of Michael, I was able to relax and have the best show of my life."

"What was your mother thinking with bringing Michael back? Is she intentionally trying to sabotage you? I can't believe she did that even after you told her not to. Have you talked to her since the show?" Ainsley asks before taking a sip of champagne.

I shake my head and down my entire glass. "No, and I don't want to. I'm still so pissed at her that I don't know if I'll be able to keep my cool and not fire her for what she did tonight."

"Really?" my life coach asks in utter shock. "You wouldn't really fire Andrea, would you? I mean, she's not only your manager. She's your mother."

"Then she should act like either one of those goddamned things. She didn't do her job as my manager tonight, that's for damn sure. As for acting like my mother, well, she hasn't been good at that job for a long time."

I stop myself before I get too upset again. I can't think about my mother's antics tonight. I want to stay in this good mood for when I go to speak to Liam in a little while, and everything about my mother's behavior will only make me angry again.

Holding out my glass for Ainsley to refill, I force myself to smile and forget about all of the madness. "Tonight isn't for that. Tonight is to celebrate a great show, and that's what I'm doing. My mother will have to wait until tomorrow."

Wiggling her eyebrows again, Ainsley gives me a knowing smile. "So what are you planning to do to celebrate?"

I look around at the group of people who've been with me through thick and thin and then back at her. "This? You act like I have some secret plans to do something else, Ains. This is it. I'm going to finish this glass of champagne and then I'm going to take a hot bath full of bubbles. And if I don't fall asleep in the tub, I'm going to relax with a mud mask on my face because I swear to God my skin felt like it was blowing up with zits under all that makeup tonight. It's been a while since I had to wear that much."

"You looked gorgeous, just in case you're thinking you didn't."

Something about the way she says that makes me curious, so I ask, "Why would I think anything else?"

She shrugs, but since she's Ainsley, she can't help but tell me what's on her mind. "I just thought maybe someone had said something negative about how you have to look for when you're on stage."

I know what she's saying, but she's wrong. Liam never said a word about how I looked. I'm not even sure he noticed.

"Well, you're wrong. Nobody said a thing about my makeup or the quantity I had to wear tonight."

Holding her hands up in front of her, she pretends to surrender on this point. "Okay, fine. I just wanted to make sure that you know you look beautiful no matter how much makeup you wear."

"Why do you always think the worst of him?" I ask, startling her with my very pointed question.

"I don't."

"Yes, you do. You never have a nice thing to say about him, and now you're accusing him of making me feel bad about wearing stage makeup when I never said a word about him even mentioning it. You know, I have thoughts of my own. I can decide that my face feels gross with all of that covering my skin all on my own."

I see I've hit a nerve when her expression shows how hurt she is by my words. "I wasn't trying to say that at all. I know you can make your own decisions. You might forget, but I'm a big fan of you doing that. I have been since the day you hired me. I'm just worried that he's got this wholesome thing in his mind about how women are and that's not you."

Instantly, I feel defensive. "Why? What has given you the impression that he's all about people being wholesome? I've never seen that in him. Liam is simply a good man. Why can't you just accept that and be happy that I like him?"

By the time I finish speaking, my voice is far too loud and everyone turns to stare at me, ceasing their conversations to pay attention to ours. Ainsley throws them all a dirty look, and they resume talking, but I know they heard me say I like Liam.

So what? I like my bodyguard. I wish everyone would stop acting like it's the crime of the century or the most scandalous thing since Catherine the Great decided to hang out with horses.

I stand up from the pool deck to leave before I start to feel as unhappy as I did when I was dealing with my mother earlier. "I'm going to go take that bath. Enjoy the party," I say, looking down at Ainsley.

"Please don't go yet, Mia. I'm sorry. I think you misinterpreted what I said, and I want to fix that," she pleads.

But it's no use.

I didn't misunderstand what she said now or every other time we talked about Liam. She doesn't like him. I don't know why, and I don't care. She doesn't have to like him.

"It's fine. No harm, no foul. I just need to go relax."

Turning to look over at everyone enjoying themselves, I raise my glass in the air and smile at them. "To a great show with great friends! Enjoy, but remember we have to do it all over again tomorrow night!"

Ainsley reaches out to grab my hand to keep me from leaving, but I pull it away as soon as she touches me. I love her and she's my best friend, but I don't want to answer any questions tonight about why I care about Liam or why I feel better when he's around.

I just do, and that's enough for me.

I SINK DOWN INTO MY NEW STANDALONE TUB FILLED with hot water and lavender bubble bath, closing my eyes as relaxation comes over me. No more talking. No more thinking. No more anything but me and this tub and the bubbles that cover my body.

While I enjoy the silence, I wonder what Liam is doing right now. He's probably hanging out with his guys going over what needs to be tweaked for tomorrow night's show. All work and no play seems to be his mantra. He should change that. I can appreciate the work he does, but a little more play would be nice.

As I imagine them all seated around the table in his room with serious faces discussing how this guy should move his position to this place and that guy should adjust where he stands by so many feet, I can't help but sigh in relief that he came to my rescue when

I needed him tonight. Michael never did that, but then again, I never knew he was doing such a shitty job protecting me that I had anything to worry about.

Nobody ever did anything like that for me before. I had no idea what I was missing.

And now that I know how good it feels, I sure as hell don't want to go back to not having that kind of feeling.

Lost in thought about Liam, I don't realize my hand has slid down my slick skin until my finger strokes between my legs for the first time. Mmmm... God, that feels good. I haven't been with any man in far too long, and although my hand and vibrators do the trick, they aren't usually as good as the real thing.

Now, though, as I close my eyes and imagine him between my legs lashing my pussy with his tongue, I can't help but notice this is much better than usual. Every inch of my body feels alive, like every nerve ending is wide awake and firing on all cylinders. It must be the subject matter of tonight's fantasy.

I can see him in my mind's eye without a shirt on, his hard, muscular body settled in between my thighs as he goes down on me better than any man ever has. I stuff my hand into his hair and run my fingers through it. Softer than I thought it would be, it feels like silk against my skin.

His thumbs hold me open so he can reach every delicious spot on me. Deep inside, the first tendrils of my orgasm begin to unravel, and with every inch the sensation travels, a feeling of utter ecstasy comes with it.

Finally, he sucks my clit gently into between his lips, and that's all it takes. Colors and shapes explode behind my eyes, and it's like every inch of my body is turned toward my pussy to watch it revel in how incredible this feels.

I smile at that fantasy, and a second later, my finger dips inside me as I come harder than I think I've ever done before in my life from masturbating. My legs shoot out until the soles of my feet slam against the wall of the tub, and I cry out in utter pleasure.

Exhausted, I slide down under the water until my whole body is submerged. Oh, God, I hope that fantasy comes true and he's as good as I dream he is. If he doesn't know how to do me better than my own hand, I think I might be depressed for a month.

A knocking noise rips me out of my thoughts of Liam going down on me, and I pop up above the surface of the water to listen to where it's coming from. Pushing my hair back off my face, I look around for any clue. It's not here in the bathroom. That's for sure.

I strain to hear it and realize a few seconds later it's someone knocking on my bedroom door. Probably Ainsley. She hates when we have disagreements, and I did leave her pretty abruptly. She probably wants to make sure we aren't really fighting.

"Come in!" I yell and then look down my body to assess the bubble situation. There's still enough for Ainsley to come talk to me.

As I slide my hands up over the top of my head to get a few stray hairs stuck near my eyes, I hear her come in. Now that I've calmed down and relaxed in the bath a little, I don't feel so much like going toe to toe with her about Liam. She'll come around to see how great he is. She just needs some time.

Ainsley doesn't say anything at first, so I look over toward the door to see why she's so silent. It's very much not like her to not start talking the second she walks into my room.

But when I turn my head, it isn't my life coach I see leaning against the doorframe but Liam! His arms are folded across his broad chest, and the white T-shirt he's wearing seems to strain against his biceps. I look up at his face to see him smiling, and for a second, I smile back.

Until I realize I barely had enough bubbles a few minutes ago. Now, I don't have enough to cover the major parts of my body, leaving much of me exposed.

"Liam, what are you doing here? I thought you were Ainsley!" I say as I scramble to cross my arms over my chest.

He doesn't look away, even as I splash around all flustered that he's watching me naked in the tub. "I just wanted to come by and check on you after all that happened tonight."

Something about the lilt of his voice tells me he's enjoying how bothered his being here makes me. That and the fact that he hasn't stopping grinning since I first noticed him.

"I'm fine. Slightly unbubbled, but fine all the same."

Finally, his smile fades, and he asks, "Unbubbled?"

I drop my gaze to the bath quickly becoming merely water with almost no bubbles and then look up at him. "Unbubbled. As in, there were a lot more bubbles just a few minutes ago. Why don't you wait for me out in my room and we can talk as soon as I get dried off."

His smile returns, and I'm sure he can see right into my bathtub from the angle he's staring down at me. "It's okay. We can talk tomorrow. I just wanted to check on you."

For a moment, my embarrassment fades, and I feel nothing but happy that someone cared enough to see if I was okay after all that happened at the show tonight. I want to talk to him, so I say, "Please wait for me. I'll be right out. Just close the door and I swear it won't take long."

"Okay."

When the door clicks closed, I hurry to get out of the tub and grab one of my favorite white towels off the stand a few feet away. After a quick drying-off, I slip into my white robe that's made of the softest Egyptian cotton and rush toward the door.

Oh, God! I might look like a disaster. Ainsley was concerned about him saying something about my wearing a ton of makeup for the show, but now I don't have a stitch of anything on my face. I'm probably all blotchy from the heat of the bath too.

I take a look at myself in the mirror and see things aren't terrible. I wish I had some makeup on my eyes, though. They always look better with some dark eyeshadow to highlight the dark brown color of my eyes. Surprisingly, the rest of my face doesn't look too shabby, thankfully.

With a quick swipe of my tongue across my lips, I give them a little sheen and smile at my reflection. My heart's racing, and I feel like I might crumble to the floor I'm so nervous.

"Relax," I say to the me in the mirror. "You're great. This is fine."

I give myself one final smile and turn to walk toward the door. If I'm so great, though, why am I shaking like a leaf?

CHAPTER NINE

ia

I TAKE A DEEP BREATH AS I WALK TOWARD WHERE Liam sits on the edge of my bed. He looks like he's ready to bolt at any second. Maybe I've been reading all the signals I thought were coming off him wrong? I was so sure he felt something for me.

"Okay, now I feel much better. A bath can do a girl a world of good."

He nods like he agrees, but I get the feeling he's not a bath guy. Maybe he would be if he had the right woman?

Sitting down next to him, I wonder where the smiling Liam who stood gawking at me in my bathroom a few minutes ago has gone. Now he seems uncomfortable, but that doesn't make any sense.

"So tonight was exciting, huh?" I say with a smile and hope he gives me on in return.

He glances over at me and nods. "Definitely more exciting than I had expected," he says quietly.

Then he looks away, like he can't stand to see the sight of me.

"Is there something wrong, Liam? You're acting strange."

I don't want to sound like his behavior is hurting me, but it comes through loud and clear. Is it that I don't have any makeup on and my hair is still sopping wet? Is he disappointed by how I look now?

That can't be it. I looked pretty much like this when I was in the bathtub a few minutes ago.

He doesn't turn to look at me when he says, "Your robe."

"What about it?" I ask, wondering if this guy has some irrational hatred of Egyptian cotton or white robes.

I watch his expression as he winces like he's in pain before he points toward me, still not able to face me. "It's open."

Glancing down, I see my robe has come open right above my waist, so he has a clear view of my naked breasts. Horrified since he probably thinks I came out here looking like some cheap floozy hoping to get a little, I hurry to pull the parts of my robe together, covering myself up to my neck.

"Well, no surprise left with me, I guess," I say, trying desperately to make a joke of what feels like the most humiliating moment of my life. "You can look at me, Liam. Trust me. I'm so covered I look like I'm straight out of the Victorian Era over here."

When he finally turns to face me, he smiles and shakes his head. "You surprise me every day, Mia. I doubt that's going to change just because you flashed me."

I feel heat flood my cheeks at his words. Slapping his arm, I protest, "I did not flash you. Man, a girl doesn't tie her robe tight enough and a guy thinks she's flashing him. Trust me. If I flashed you, you would have gotten more than a little peek at my boobs."

This is not how I wanted this conversation to go. I had hoped we could talk a little so I could thank him again for coming to my rescue tonight, and then we could kiss. I didn't have the whole thing planned out, but it certainly didn't look like what's happening now when I imagined it.

When I see his face turn red, at least I know I'm not the only one feeling completely awkward here. Something about him being embarrassed too charms me, though. That's probably the uptight side of him. Not my favorite side, but if it's the part that blushes, I could get used to it.

"So now that we're both feeling weird, I wanted to thank you for what you did tonight, Liam. Nobody has ever bothered to worry about me like you do. I know it's your job, but still, nobody else has ever done your job like you do."

"I'm happy to do whatever it takes to make sure you're safe."

I watch his mouth as he says that and all I can think of is how much I want to kiss him right now. Well, that and how good he looks in that white T-shirt. Who knew a man could make a plain white shirt look so hot?

"I mean it when I say no one has ever taken care of me like you, Liam. I mean, my security."

My tiny slip makes his eyes get slightly wider for a second, and I think maybe he's going to make a move. I stare into his blue eyes that never fail to amaze me with how gorgeous they are, but he doesn't budge.

"I'll find out what happened with your mother and make sure it doesn't happen again tomorrow night. I plan on telling her when we head to New Orleans that Michael isn't welcome to come along."

The mention of my former head of security makes me feel nothing but shame. I hang my head to avoid Liam's gaze, hating how I used to rely on Michael for so much when he cared nothing about my safety or happiness.

"What's wrong?" he asks, his voice full of the concern that I love hearing in him. "I need to tell your mother she can't pull that kind of thing again, Mia. She put you in danger, and I can't have that."

I look up at him and shake my head. "It's not that. Feel free to tell my mother whatever you need to. I'm just so embarrassed that I believed Michael cared about me or keeping me safe."

Liam's expression hardens, and his eyes narrow to almost angry slits. "How serious were you two?" he asks.

"We weren't. Did he claim we did something together? Because we didn't. We weren't like that. I thought he cared for me at least as a friend, but you saw the proof of how wrong I was about that when you went to his apartment looking for me."

He shakes his head as his expression softens. "He didn't say anything to me. We weren't exactly on speaking terms tonight."

"Then why do you think we were together?"

Liam doesn't answer, and suddenly I wonder if he believes I sleep with all of my bodyguards. I need him to know that isn't true at all. In fact, I've never slept with any of them.

Oh, God! I see it in his eyes. That's what he thinks!

"You think I just sleep with every guy who guards me?"

"No. I thought you slept with him, though. The way you were acting when you went to see him that day seemed like how someone would act if they were serious with someone."

I shake my head faster and faster as how Liam's acted all makes sense to me now. "No, Liam I've never slept with Michael or any of my bodyguards. That's not how it is. Is that why you've been so strange with me every time I show you I care for you?"

He abruptly stands up from the bed and shakes his head. I stare up at him in confusion and think to myself that we're like a couple of deranged bobblehead dolls.

"Why did you get up?"

"I should go," he says flatly, like all the emotion has left him suddenly.

"Why? What did I say wrong? I told you that Michael and I were never together. I've never been with anyone guarding me. Isn't that a good thing?"

Worry now seems etched into his beautiful features as he continues to shake his head like nothing I'm saying makes him happy. "It's not that, Mia."

I jump to my feet, needing to stop him if he moves to leave. "Then what is it? Because the way you're acting doesn't make any sense. You stand there in the doorway to my bathroom staring at me naked in the tub, but then you get weird when my robe comes open. You bring up Michael, and then when I tell you he was never anyone romantic to me, you grow cold, but I could have sworn you were upset at the thought that he and I were together. Why are you acting like this? I don't understand."

Still, he doesn't answer me. "I should go."

I grab his hand, feeling instantly better when I touch him. Even his fingers possess strength I don't think I could ever even dream of having. They're long and heavy in my palm, but I cling to them when he takes a step toward the door.

"Please don't go. Tell me what I did wrong, Liam. I've tried to show you I'm not that brat you thought I was or the diva you accused me of being. I thought I was doing everything right to make you see that I care about you, and I thought you cared about me. Was I wrong?"

He won't look at me now, turning away as he lets

out a heavy sigh. "No, you weren't wrong. I've noticed it all. I see I misjudged you at first. I get why all those people come to see you. It's not just that you're an incredible singer. The person you were on stage tonight is the person I've seen so many times here at the house."

"Then why do you want to leave and why won't you face me if I'm so wonderful?"

I don't care that I sound desperate. I'm not, but I know he probably thinks I am. What I am is a woman who cares who wants to know if he cares about me in return.

Maybe I am desperate. All I know is I've never felt anything like I do when Liam's around me.

Finally, after what feels like an eternity, he turns around. In his eyes, I see all that emotion I had hoped he felt for me coloring those beautiful blue eyes of his. But his mouth is turned down in a frown that makes me think those emotions aren't the ones I had hoped to find in him.

"This can't happen. I'm to blame, so I take full responsibility for this. I shouldn't have stood in your doorway for so long watching you in the tub. I'm sorry about that."

God, I hate seeing him so unhappy!

I tighten my hold on his hand, sure he's about to leave before I can say another word. "You don't have to be sorry. I'm not. It's okay. You didn't do anything wrong."

He stares down into my eyes and says, "Yes, I did. I live by a code that's meant I kept a sharp line between me and my clients. Until you, I never had a problem respecting that line that kept me over here and everyone else over there. But I've stepped over that line, blurred it, and even tried to forget it existed because you make me want to do things I shouldn't."

"Why shouldn't you want to feel someone care about you? Why wouldn't you want to care about me?"

"Because it goes against everything I believe in."

"So you won't let yourself feel something you already know you feel for me?"

I wait for him to answer me, to tell me what I want to believe is true. That he does feel something for me like I do for him.

But he says nothing.

My father used to tell me that if you want things in life, you have to take a chance. He didn't seem to believe in that mantra when it came to my wanting to be a star, but I never forgot him telling me that when I was a little girl and my family was still something I had in my life.

I have to take a chance now. If it all goes bad, then at least I'll know that I took a chance at having the kind of man in my life that I've always sung about.

Someone strong who would stand against anyone who wanted to hurt me. A man who would brave the winds of a hurricane to protect me. I want that man, and since he's standing here in front of me, there's no time like the present.

So I stand up on my tiptoes to reach his mouth and kiss him with every ounce of desire coursing through me. My eyes closed, I don't know what he's doing as I move my lips against his. At first, he feels stiff, almost like a statue I'm trying to wake from its cold slumber, but slowly, his mouth softens and then he returns my kiss with one of his own as full of need and passion as mine and I'm suddenly soaring my heart is so full.

Liam's left arm wraps around my body, pulling me to him, and for the first time, I realize how much larger than me he is. I've always had to look up at him since I'm shorter, but pressed against me, his body is like that of a giant's.

Opening my eyes, I see his face close to mine filling my gaze. He leans back, breaking our kiss, and smiles as he lets out a heavy sigh.

"So much for that sharp line."

I lift my hand to his mouth and press my fingertip to the center of those delicious lips. "I didn't like that line anyway."

He gives me a big smile in return that makes this night the best night of my life. Then it fades, and I wonder if I'm going to need to kiss him again to calm all those unnecessary worries he has.

Ainsley is right. Liam really is Mr. Rules and Regulations.

"What's wrong? I swear to God, I will throw you down on that bed and make you smile again," I say with a laugh.

"It's nothing, but what do you think about keeping this to ourselves? You may be used to the whole world knowing your every move, but I'm not."

He's got a point. To be honest, the last thing I want

to have to deal with is the nosy press snooping around if they find out I'm with someone new. I've worked hard to make sure that the only time my name appears in the press is because of my talent.

Or when I run off and my mother makes it a media circus. But those days are behind me now that I'm with Liam.

I kiss him sweetly on the lips and smile. "Our secret. Just you and me."

CHAPTER TEN

iam

THE SECOND SHOW AT THE PAVILION WENT OFF without a hitch, and since that first night, Andrea has kept her distance from me, making herself practically invisible around the house and anywhere near Mia. I expected her to make an appearance today since we left for the first big show in New Orleans, but she wasn't to be found. I thought maybe she decided to hide out on one of the other tour busses, but neither the band nor the dancers saw her at all.

All night I've kept an eye out for her and Michael, just in case she wanted to try to pull something, even as I watched out for any of the more rabid fans of Mia's. In between that and making sure every one of my men and the local security were in their places, I've tried to sneak a few moments to watch her perform.

The arena falls almost silent and the lights dim until only a single spotlight shines on her in the center of the stage. Behind her, the guy who plays keyboards sits at a grand piano playing a sad melody. When she begins singing, I feel like someone's stolen my breath away with how beautiful yet mournful the words are. She told me she writes all her songs, and as I listen to her sing about losing someone dear to her, I wonder who this one is about.

Whoever he is, he has no idea how lucky he is to have her write this song about him.

I pull myself away from watching her when it sounds like each word she's singing is filled with tears, turning around and seeing Drew staring at me. Instantly, my senses go on high alert. Is something wrong? Does he see something we need to handle?

Hurrying over to where he stands off left center stage, I grab him by the arm to get his attention. "What's going on? Is there something we need to deal with?"

A slow smile lights up his face. "I don't know. You tell me."

"What the hell does that mean? I need to know if there's anything we need to pay attention to, Drew. What's with the riddles?"

He tilts his head toward Mia out on stage and shrugs. "No riddles. I'm just wondering about what I was seeing a minute ago."

I still have no idea what the hell he's talking about, but if there's some danger I'm not seeing, he needs to let me know now and stop with this bullshit.

"What? Was someone trying to get close to the stage? Those local guys have been good all night. What happened?"

Jesus, my heart is racing like someone's chasing me. I need to calm down if I'm going to handle some problem he's about to point out to me.

Drew slugs me in the shoulder and laughs. "Not that, you jackass. I'm talking about you watching her like she's some angel sent from heaven. You got it bad, man. I can see it as clear as day."

So much for keeping this thing between us a secret.

"Damn. I thought I was being cool too. How obvious is it?" I ask, dreading the answer he's about to give me.

Grinning, he says, "Well, I guess if someone's blind they wouldn't know. It's not like any of the other guys have said anything, but if they've been watching you like I was, they have to know something's up."

I pinch the bridge of my nose, angry at myself for being so careless. "Okay, do me a favor. Don't say a word about this to anyone. If any of the guys say anything, I want you to blow it off like you think they're crazy. Or if you can't do that, just send them to me and I'll do it."

Drew and I are tight, but he isn't the kind of person to lie to others. I'm putting him in an awkward position with the rest of the crew. He shouldn't have to do that.

Before he can say anything, I shake my head and reverse what I just told him. "Forget that. I shouldn't be asking you to lie to people. That's a shitty thing to do to a friend. Sorry about that."

"It's cool. I don't need to tell other people your business. Hell, you didn't have to admit the truth to me, so let's just pretend I know nothing and I'll funnel any questions your way. Word to the wise, though. Stop mooning over this woman in public or everyone on the goddamned planet is going to know what's going on between you two."

I grab his hand to shake it, thankful for his suggestion. "I'll definitely do that. And here I thought Mia was going to be the one who would blow our cover."

When she finds out I'm to blame for someone else knowing, she's never going to let me hear the end of it.

ALONE IN MY HOTEL ROOM, I WAIT FOR MIA TO finish her after-performance routine with her entourage. Now that Drew told me he knows about us, I have to let her know. The only problem is I don't know how to do that.

Pacing back and forth, I look out the window at the French Quarter below with every pass. It's been a bunch of years since I got to enjoy New Orleans. The last time I was here it was Cash, Alex, Cade, and me celebrating Alex's twenty-first birthday. That was a weekend to remember, except we partied so much I only vaguely recall arriving at the first bar on Bourbon Street and waking up on Sunday in the hotel room with the headache to beat all headaches.

When I walk back to the door, I hear three knocks, Mia's made up code to let me know it's her. I open it up without looking out the peephole and immediately chastise myself for not following even that most basic of protocols.

This woman has me turned upside down.

She rushes into the room, and I slam the door behind her. When I turn around, I'm met with a look I hadn't expected. Instead of her brown hair, she has platinum blond hair about three inches shorter than what she usually has. She's also dressed in the tiniest black dress I've ever seen with four-inch heels dangling off the fingers on her right hand and a little red purse hanging off her left wrist.

"Do you like it? It's my disguise. I got it from Crystal. I want to go out into the French Quarter and have a good time tonight. What do you say?" she asks, practically bursting from excitement.

Still trying to get used to her new appearance, I smile. "Sounds good, but did you forget something?"

For a second she stops bouncing up and down in front of me and thinks about what she may have forgotten. "I don't think so. Wig for disguise. I've got money. Sexy bodyguard to protect me. Nope. I got it all covered."

I take a step toward her and lean down to kiss her. "You're not twenty-one, Mia. No one is going to let you into a bar without ID."

Although this would seem like an insurmountable challenge, she waves it off like it's nothing. "Ridiculous. You can walk around drinking right on the streets in this city. Do you honestly think anyone is checking people to make sure they're of age? Anyway, I have ID."

"That says you're nineteen."

Juggling the shoes and the purse, she whips out a small plastic card and holds it in front of her. "Wrong again. I have Ainsley's. She let me borrow it. So you have no more excuses. Let's go!"

Remembering the reason why my job guarding her happened later than it was supposed to, I quietly ask, "Do you think going to a bar is a good idea? I mean, since you're not that long out of rehab?"

Mia shakes her head and laughs. "Don't worry about that."

Hoping to put off having to worry about anything dealing with heading out into public, I slide my good arm around her waist and pull her to me. "What do you say to postponing our tour of the French Quarter for a while?"

She smiles up at me as her eyebrows slowly raise into her forehead. "Oh? Do you have something you want us to do instead?"

Looking around at the private suite I've been given for tonight, I smile. "I just figured since your suite is filled with all those people, this could be a good time for us to finally be alone."

"Alone alone?" she asks in a surprised voice.

I nod. "Yes."

Suddenly, Mia narrows her eyes and gets a suspicious look on her face. "You know I'm all in on sleeping with you, Liam. I have been since that first night we kissed. You're the one who's been saying we should keep this on the down low and hasn't wanted to be alone alone because everyone's been around. So what's changed?"

Time to fess up. But first, I need her to know I've been all in on sleeping with her for all that time too.

"Well, before I tell you the reason, I want you to understand I wasn't trying to hold out on us being together for any reason but the one I said. I'm not really into public romances, so I was hoping one of these nights we'd finally be alone. Tonight's a perfect time for that since everyone's already drunk up in your suite."

She smiles up at me like she sees right through my attempt to soften the news I have to give her. "Okay. Good to know that you wanted to have sex and this waiting business wasn't because you didn't find me desirable."

Christ. This is going south fast.

I take her face in my hands and kiss her on the center of her beautiful mouth. "Of course I do. I'm just not used to being crazy about a woman who has an entourage around her at all times."

"Point taken," she says with a nod. "But there's another reason you're suddenly feeling that this night in the New Orleans Ritz Carlton is the perfect time for us to be together for the first time. So what is it?"

With a sigh, I hang my head and confess the truth. "Drew knows. He told me tonight. I wanted to keep our being together quiet, and I was the one who blew it."

"He saw you doing that moony-eyed thing you do when I'm on stage, didn't he?" she says with a giggle.

I look up and see she's not angry. Good. I'm still pissed at myself for being so transparent, but at least she's not.

"Yeah," I say, nodding as I admit my idiocy. "I had no idea I looked at you like that. I'm usually pretty stoic. At least that's what I've been told."

"Well, Drew seems like a guy who can keep a secret." In a flash, worry fills her eyes. "You did tell him to keep this to himself, didn't you?"

"Absolutely and he is. Drew's a good guy."

Mia shrugs and lifts herself up onto her toes to kiss me. "Then it's all good. You are going to have to practice looking at me like you don't give a damn, though, or everyone's going to know we're together by the end of the week."

"I'll see what I can do."

She trails her fingertips down the column of my neck and begins to unbutton my black shirt. "For what it's worth, I love seeing you look at me like that. I don't think anyone has ever actually looked like you do when you watch me sing."

"Moony-eyed?" I joke as she makes her way down my shirt.

Nodding, she looks up at me and gives me one of her beautiful smiles. "Yeah. I wish you didn't have to stop. It makes me feel better than I can even explain, Liam."

As she slides her hands under my shirt and down over my left shoulder, I shrug out of it as much as I can and lean down to kiss her. "How about I find something else that makes you feel that way?"

Her gaze roams over my half-naked body, and she says with a soft sigh, "Mmmm...I like the way you think."

Glancing over at my right arm, I smile as I start to slide the sling off my shoulder. "Just give me a second or two and I'll be good to go."

CHAPTER ELEVEN

ia

I'VE BEEN DYING TO BE WITH LIAM SINCE THAT FIRST
night we realized we didn't want to fight our attraction
anymore. He wanted to take things easy and wait until
we could spend some time alone, but if it had been up
to me, I would have slept with him that night. His
ability to control his desires impresses me, but at some
point, control needs to go out the window.

So I'm rarely ever alone. That's my life. Any man
who wants to be with me has to get used to that. Liam
will. He's a great guy and smart. He'll figure out how
to get around the entourage.

My heart thumps in my chest as anticipation tears
through me. I love looking at Liam's body. At least the
half of it I've seen naked before. And tonight's no
exception. As my hands roam over his muscular chest

and shoulders down to his thick biceps, all I can think about it how beautiful he is.

Then I suddenly realize I touched where the bullet entered his arm and quickly pull my hand back toward me. "I'm sorry. I didn't mean to just brush over your arm like that."

Smiling, he lifts his right arm and moves it around to prove to me he's fine. "No problem. That doctor was probably being extra careful because I feel one hundred percent. See?"

"Okay. I just wanted to be sure."

"Is that the way I look at you?" he asks with a chuckle, thankfully changing the subject. "No wonder Drew caught me. I guess I should be happy very few people pay attention to me because if they did, they'd all know."

My cheeks heat from a blush and I smile up at him. "Maybe."

I move my hands down his body to begin removing his belt and pants. "Now no more talking about the two of us and our moony-eyes. I need to get you naked."

"What about you?" he asks with such a tone of innocence that I have to tear my focus away from my job getting him undressed to see if he's serious. I look up and see he's absolutely for real. Clearly, Liam isn't used to someone like me.

"Well, this dress I'm wearing offers easy access, but I've made it even easier by not wearing any underwear. You're welcome, by the way."

His blue eyes get wide in surprise, and I swear he

looks downright sweet at this moment. "Really? I guess you had this all planned out. So we were never going out into the Quarter tonight?"

"Oh, yeah. I just figured we'd end up doing something like this in a dark alley way."

Again, surprise makes his eyes open wide. He opens his mouth to say something, but nothing comes out, so I stand on my toes and kiss him. "Now let me get these pants off you or we're never going to have any fun tonight."

Liam pushes my hands away from his body and hurriedly unbuttons his pants. A few seconds later, he shoves them down his legs and kicks them away across the room. "Problem solved."

He's still partially dressed in his black boxer briefs and black socks, so I point at both and shake my head. "There is no way I can have sex with a man who's wearing socks. Take them off."

For a second, he looks like he's going to protest, but then he bends down to slide them off his feet. Looking up at me with a wickedness in his eyes, he points at my dress. "Take it off. The first time we sleep together, I'm not doing it dark alley style."

I giggle, loving how cute he can be. "Deal."

By the time I slither out of my teeny-tiny black dress I had my personal shopper specially get for tonight, Liam is fully naked and staring at me with those moony-eyes I love. I doubt he loves my body as much as I love his as I stand there taking in every gorgeous inch of him. Damn, he's like a Greek god chiseled out of the finest marble and all for me.

When he doesn't make a move for a few seconds, a flash of insecurity takes over. My body isn't anywhere as perfect as his. No matter how many workouts and routines Mitchell and Tiffany put me through, I never get my body into the shape Liam's is in.

It's why all my costumes are made to hide the softness of my abs and highlight my best part. My legs. The designers do an incredible job, but at this moment, I can't hide behind sequins and a great dress.

"Better tell Mitchell I need more crunches, huh?" I mumble.

Liam shakes his head and steps toward me to cradle my face in his hands. Gazing down into my eyes, he smiles and I feel like my entire body is melting.

"No. You're perfect just as you are. Don't change a single thing."

Oh. No one's ever said that or anything close to that to me.

"I just thought that since you're so built that you might have hoped I was."

Again, he shakes his head. "I don't want a woman who's the female version of me. I like this version of you instead."

I can't help but close my eyes. He feels too close, too much surrounding me at this moment. How is it he's single? He's gorgeous, sweet, caring, and protective. And right now, his long, hard cock is pressing against the space between my hipbones and driving me wild. Women must be climbing over one another to get to him, yet here he is with me.

"What's wrong, Mia?" he asks in a low voice.

Opening my eyes, I shake my head. "Nothing. Nothing at all." I don't know why, but I can't stop myself from asking how it's possible he's single. "How is it you don't have someone already?"

When he gives me one of those sexy smiles and subtly tilts his hips to press his body against mine, it's like someone's sucked all the air out of the room. I wait breathlessly for him to say something, and then he does, and it's the best thing in the world.

"I do. You."

He doesn't give me a chance to respond before he kisses me and once again takes my breath away. His mouth is soft but insistent, like he's a man who knows how to give a woman pleasure but also will take what he wants. It's a combination that turns me on more than I ever thought possible.

My hands slide over his soft skin as I silently worship how perfect his body is. I've never been with anyone like Liam, and it's all I can do to not stand here in the center of this hotel suite and admire every beautiful inch of him.

When he cups my breasts in his palms and presses his cock against my belly, I swear I get so hot I might come before we get past foreplay. Something about his strength and protective nature mixed with this body makes me more excited than I've ever been before with any man.

I break our kiss and smile up at him as my hands continue their exploration with his washboard abs.

"You are perfect. I swear I could run my hands over your body all night long."

"The beauty of weights and working out, although genetics might contribute to it too."

All of this and humble too.

"I was feeling a little insecure there when I saw you with no clothes on. I mean, I knew you had a great body, but I guess just seeing it naked surprised me," I mumble, suddenly shy about what I truly want.

What I've wanted from the moment I realized I cared about him.

"Then I guess we're both feeling pretty stunned right now because every fantasy I made up in my head about you pales in comparison to seeing you here with me right now."

Jesus. Even if this man is terrible in bed, I might just have to stay with him because he's so perfect in every other way.

But there's no way he's going to be anything less than phenomenal.

Reaching between our bodies, I wrap my fingers around his thick cock and stroke him up to the top. "I've fantasized about you and me together since the first time you kissed me. I can't wait to see if I was anywhere close with what I came up with."

Dipping his head, he whispers in my ear in the sexiest voice, "I'll do my best."

He lifts me by the waist and carries me over to the bed, placing me gently on the down comforter. It's soft against my skin, like a cloud cradling me ever so tenderly as he looms above me, staring down into my eyes with utter need.

Liam slides up my body, exciting nerve endings every inch of the way until his mouth reaches mine and he kisses me hard. I lift my legs and wrap them around his waist, rubbing my feet over his ass as I make my way up to his waist. God, even his ass is toned!

Pressing my heels into the small of his back, I urge him on, but he doesn't need any convincing. With one slow thrust, he fills me completely, yet again taking my breath away. Jesus, he's much bigger than I'm used to, so it's like I can't move without his permission.

I've never felt this way during sex. Usually, I'm the one who likes to set the pace, but with his hips pinning mine to the bed, I have no choice but to give in so Liam can decide how fast or how slowly we go.

I lazily slide my hands down over his back, reveling in the feel of his taut muscles with every time he thrusts his hips and sinks into me again. He's the personification of power and restraint both at once. I sense he wants to let himself go, but I'm so much smaller than he is and he probably thinks I can't take it.

But I want to. I want all he has to give me. I want every delicious inch of him giving me all he has.

So I press my heels harder into the base of his spine and drag my nails across his broad shoulders. In his ear, I moan, "Don't hold back, Liam. I want all of you."

He stops for a few seconds and looks down at me,

his eyes filled with need and desire. "I don't want to hurt you."

"You won't. You would never hurt me. I know that," I say, gently cupping his face.

As he covers my mouth in a kiss, he pushes into me hard, hitting a place inside that I never knew excited before this moment. His cock presses against that spot, sending me into overdrive just as he begins to fuck me in earnest.

I cling to him, riding every thrust and giving him all I have in me. We're savage and raw, and I feel like my emotions threaten to tear me apart at the seams. I don't have to worry about if he sees me fall to pieces like other men, though. This is Liam, the man who protects me, even when I don't want to be protected.

This is the man who looks at me with eyes full of love when I sing, not knowing that every word I sing now is about him.

When I feel that exquisite twinge that tells me I'm about to come, I dig my nails into his back and moan, "Don't stop! This feels so fucking good!"

He rears back at my angry raking across his skin and plunges into me just as I begin to come. An explosion of color erupts behind my eyes, and then it's like I'm hundreds of feet in the air, soaring above everything that always worries and stresses me, safe in the arms of the man I know would never put me in harm's way.

I feel his body flood mine in warmth, and then he stills, holding himself so he doesn't put all his weight on me. I let out a heavy sigh, satisfied and happier than I've been in a long time.

"Hell of a first time," I say with a tiny giggle.

He nods and smiles as a dreamy look comes over him. "I'd say. I'm not usually surprised by people, but you surprised me."

"You said I surprise you every day. I really think you should have seen this coming, no pun intended."

With another nod, he admits the truth he told me just recently. "You do. I guess I just wasn't prepared for you to surprise me when we had sex."

I move out from underneath him and lie on my side, holding my head up with my hand. "Thought I'd be this tiny little thing in bed. After all the times I've stood toe to toe with you, you actually thought I'd be some dainty little thing when I have sex?"

Liam collapses to the bed and lies on his side, mirroring what I'm doing. Staring into my eyes, he smiles. "Your smallness confused me. I guess I wasn't expecting that much oomph."

The way he describes what I assume was all that scratching I did on his back makes me laugh. "Sorry about what I did with my nails. I bet your back looks like a wild animal got to you."

Wincing, he smiles. "I don't know. How's it look?" he asks before rolling over onto his other side.

Just as I suspected, his skin looks like something with very sharp nails came at him with an intent to shred him up. "Let's just say that if you decide to walk around not wearing a shirt within the next week or so, then someone's going to ask if you had a good time."

He rolls onto his back and shakes his head. "I guess it's T-shirts for me then because I'm not a fan of having to lie."

I look down at him lying there with the evidence of our great sex written all over his back and can't believe he's for real. "So let me get this straight. You're gorgeous, built like a Greek god, super sexy, great in bed, hung like a horse, and you don't like to lie? You must be too good to be true."

Liam gives me a sexy grin and says, "You missed great at my job."

"Which only makes you more unbelievable."

He pulls me over on top of him and kisses me, his tongue sliding against mine in a way that makes me want him for a second time. I don't care if he's too good to be true. Maybe a girl deserves that once in a while. After having too rotten to deal with and too shitty to stand, I'm happy to have someone like Liam.

Placing his hands on my hips, he sits me on his lap and I feel his cock press hard against my ass. "We can discuss how wonderful I am later. For now, this Greek god with a cock like a horse wants to see you ride me cowgirl style."

I roll my eyes. "I should have never told you those things. They're already going to your head."

As he lifts his hips up off the bed, I get up on my knees to position myself so he can slide into my needy pussy. I slowly lower myself down onto him until he's fully inside me, filling me completely.

I look down at him smiling and say, "Then again, maybe since they're the truth, that's okay."

With his hands holding me, he begins to move me up and down on him, and I see it's Liam who'll be setting the pace for sex once more. For all those perfect parts of him, there's one I haven't mentioned yet.

He's strong enough to protect me, but Alpha enough to take control of me in bed. I love that and would love to tell him, but then he might think he can control me all the time.

I can't have that.

Better to keep how much I love the way he fucks me to myself until he realizes there are places a woman wants to be dominated and places she needs to control all on her own. For now, all I want to do is enjoy how good his cock feels and how incredible he looks lying there watching me ride him.

CHAPTER TWELVE

iam

HAND IN HAND, MIA AND I WALK DOWN BOURBON Street, getting lost in the crowds out on a Tuesday night in the French Quarter. Neon lights of blue, green, yellow, and red and old fashioned street lights erase the darkness of a moonless night, but as much as this area often has a carnival vibe to it, tonight it feels like the only place in the world I want to be.

I know that's because of the woman whose delicate hand I hold in mine. Mia points at a sign for a bar and tugs on my arm to move me toward it across the street, but she runs into a man standing in her way. For a moment, my body goes on red alert when he turns to look at her with pure drunken anger in his eyes and an expression that says he wants to hit someone for daring to walk into him.

Then he tilts his head back slightly and looks up at me. I stare down at him with an unspoken warning in my eyes.

Don't say a word, buddy. This is not a woman you want to fuck with. Not tonight. Not any night.

It only takes him a second or two to figure out he'd be messing with the wrong couple, so he turns and walks away, making a space for us to continue moving toward that bar she wants to check out. She leads the way, and when we reach the sidewalk in front of the door, she turns around to smile at me.

"That guy was thinking he'd go all he-man on me. Then he got a look at you, and I think he might have pissed his pants. No wonder things go to your head. You didn't even have to say a word."

I sense admiration in her tone, and even though we're in public and we both agreed to keep the displays of affection to private, I lean down and press a tiny kiss next to her ear. "Sometimes size matters."

She laughs and her gaze slides down my body before she looks up at me again. "Size always matters, baby. The only people who say it doesn't are people who don't have it."

Nothing to disagree with there, so I point toward the door of the bar and smile. "Want to try this one?"

"Yeah."

"You know, I just realized with you in this blond wig, our first time really can't be considered our first since you're a different person," I joke.

Mia tugs at the bottom of her new blond hair and winks at me. "I do like how you think, Liam. Let's go in, have a drink, and then go back so you can have sex with the brunette me."

The man at the door doesn't give us a second glance, just as she predicted, and as she passes him, she turns to give me a knowing look. I guess my follow-the-rules personality assumes everyone is like me.

Mia isn't, though. I've known that from the first day I met her. She is definitely not a woman who's about to let herself be restrained by rules.

When we reach the bar, I give her the only seat left and stand next to her, my nature needing to protect her as much as my desire to be near her wanting to touch her. Much larger than most people around us, I wave over the bartender, a guy with his dark hair in a man bun wearing an earring in his nose.

Leaning down, I say in her ear, "What do you want to drink?"

Without answering me, she leans over the bar and says to the bartender, "We'll have a pitcher of kamikazes."

The guy looks up at me and smiles like he's in on some joke between Mia and me before turning on his heel and walking away to make our drinks. Something tells me after a pitcher of kamikazes, this won't be the Mia I sleep with either.

"Didn't I tell you no one would care that I'm not old enough?" she asks. "You worry too much, Liam. I'm thinking after a couple drinks you'll chill out. Am I right?"

I smile, happy to correct her about who I am after

a couple drinks. "Look at me. Does it look like two drinks would do anything to me? I'm thinking it would take two pitchers of kamikazes to make a dent, but tonight's not about me getting plastered. I can't do my job if I'm compromised."

The glee she's felt since we left the hotel instantly drains from her face. "So you're here as my bodyguard?" she asks in a disappointed voice.

Quickly, I answer, happy to explain what I meant. "Not at all. That doesn't change the fact that if anyone gets too close to you or tries to lay a hand on you, they're going to find out what a world of hurt feels like when a guy my size hits them and doesn't hold back."

That makes her smile again. "Okay. So they'll get to find out what it feels like to get beaten up by my boyfriend."

"Exactly."

The bartender returns with our pitcher of drinks, and before I can reach into my pocket to get my wallet out, Mia hands him a hundred. "I'm going to need another pitcher when we get low, but the rest is yours."

That handsome tip makes him grin from ear to ear, and he happily agrees to check on us to make sure we don't run low on kamikazes. As I pat my unused wallet in my front pocket, Mia pours us both a drink and holds hers up in the air.

"To boyfriends and bodyguards!"

I smile and hold my drink up to join her, saying, "I think what you did right there makes me a bodyguard while we're here."

Her face twists into a confused expression, and she shakes her head. "What do you mean? Because I paid for our drinks?"

I shrug and take a sip of kamikaze. "Call me old-fashioned."

Mia laughs and tips her glass to her mouth to take a big gulp of her drink. "I will. Liam, you are old-fashioned. Can't a woman pay for a man's drinks?"

"Sure. I guess. I just prefer to pay when I go on dates."

Leaning in toward me, she pulls my head down so she can say in my ear, "Then don't think of this as a date. Think of this as an interlude between great sessions of sex."

When she sits back in her chair and takes another sip of kamikaze, I can't help but think she's the most incredibly sexy and infuriating woman I've ever met. One minute, she's driving me crazy in bed, and the next minute, she's buying my drink at a bar and poking fun at my being old-fashioned.

I'm not sure if I want to kiss her or drag her out of this bar to explain to her how I like being that old-fashioned gentleman my parents wanted me to be. Either way, I'd still be crazy about her.

Turning to face me, she smiles and says, "You know, about that whole rehab thing. You don't have to worry. I was never in rehab."

Now I'm confused. "That's what I was told was the reason why my job working with you started late."

"That's because that's what my mother told everyone. She paid the people at Sunnybrook Rehab to say I was there detoxing, but I've never used drugs in my life. I don't have a drinking problem either."

"So where were you if you weren't in rehab?"

Mia takes a deep breath in and holds it in her lungs for a long moment before letting it out slowly, almost as if she's afraid to tell me the truth. "I was at a place where they handle depression. My mother thinks the entire world will turn away from me if they find out I'm not one hundred percent perfect all the time. It's the reason she touts me as a classical pianist when I'm really more just someone who can play the piano pretty good if I practice a lot. She's sure if the world finds out I'm bipolar that I'll suddenly be an act no one would ever want to see."

She stops for a moment before adding, "Even though I take medication for it."

Her sadness makes me wince. After seeing her perform, I can't believe her fans would abandon her for anything.

"I'm sorry."

That gets me a smile I think is genuine. "For what? You didn't make me like this."

"Not for that. Just that you have to deal with worrying you'd lose your career if people found out the truth. Maybe you could go live on social media and let your fans hear you talk about it instead of having them hear about it through the media."

Mia shakes her head. "I don't go on social media anymore. I couldn't take the horrible things people would say when I'd post, so we hired someone who looks and sounds exactly like me to handle all of that.

Some of the things they said were so cruel that I'd want to curl up into a ball and disappear. I guess to many people because I'm in the public eye, they think I don't have feelings or I couldn't see what they wrote. But I did, and it hurt."

I hate seeing her so down, so I force a smile and say, "For what it's worth, I don't think you'd lose a single fan if they found out."

Mia raises her glass and lets out a heavy sigh. "For what it's worth, I don't either, but my mother has a different opinion about this. I'll fight her on most things, but I can't find it in me to risk that she's right and I'm wrong on this one."

As I watch her down her kamikaze, I can't help but think about how Andrea has a huge effect on her daughter's life. She likes it that way too. No wonder she looked utterly stunned when I confronted her after the show that night she brought Michael back. She assumed things were going to be the way they'd always been—with everyone thinking Mia was the villain and she was the selfless hero in their story. She never thought anyone would dare to question her motives, least of all me.

But I know the truth now. I was so wrong about Mia in the beginning, but even more, I was wrong about her mother.

I DON'T KNOW HOW SHE DOES IT, BUT TWO PITCHERS of kamikazes later, of which I only had four drinks, Mia doesn't even seem slightly drunk. Afraid she might want to try for three pitchers, I suggest we hit another bar and step away from where she's sitting to encourage her to follow me.

Somehow, in those few seconds I'm not at her side, a fight breaks out right next to her between two guys who've had far too much to drink tonight. I step back to get in front of Mia to protect her, but I don't reach her in time. One of the guys gets pushed into her, and she falls to the floor, covered in the drunk's beer.

I spring into action, rushing over to pick her up before one or both of them fall on top of her. As I lift her into my arms, her blond wig slides off her head. Behind me, I hear someone say, "Hey, that's Mia," and then it's like the crowd suddenly can only focus on her and her alone out of the hundreds of people in the bar.

Hands shoot out from all directions to touch her, grabbing at her dress and her hair. She looks up at me with pure terror in her eyes, curling up into the fetal position in my arms. Never before have I seen her so frightened, and all I want to do is protect her.

I shoulder check half a dozen people as I push through the crowd toward the door. By the time I reach the street, she sobbing in my arms with her face buried in my chest.

"It's okay. I've got you. Nobody's going to hurt you. I promise."

Her terrified voice muffled by my shirt, she says, "I want to go back to the hotel, Liam. Take me back there, please."

"Okay. Just hang on to me and I'll take care of everything."

She clings to my neck like a drowning woman, but she doesn't have to fear anything now. I won't let anyone hurt her.

With each step I take toward the hotel, regret fills me for letting my guard down. If only I didn't step away from her, none of this would have ever happened.

Out of the corner of my eye, I see blood on her bare shoulder. Someone scratched her skin when they were trying to get to her, and now she's bleeding. Anger mixes with regret, and it's all I can do to not march right back to that goddamned bar and beat the hell out of everyone I recognize.

"Are we almost there?" she asks in a tiny voice.

I come out of my haze of rage and see the sign for the hotel right in front of me. "We're almost there. Don't worry. I've got you, Mia."

The guy at concierge I thought had a pretentious way of speaking when we arrived sees me walk through the front door with her in my arms and rushes over to us. Whatever affectation he had earlier has disappeared when he frantically asks in a heavy southern accent, "What happened? What do you need, Mr. Jackson?"

"She's okay, but I need to get her up to her suite immediately," I say as I hurry to the bank of elevators across the lobby.

Mia lifts her head from my chest and smiles up at me. "Would you ask him to send up something to eat? My stomach feels weird, like it needs food in it right now."

Happy to hear her sounding better, I ask, "What do you want? Whatever it is, either he'll have them make it or I'll run and get it."

Tears fill her eyes. "I'd like a pizza."

The man from concierge presses the button to summon the elevator and hears her say she wants a pizza. "I will get one sent up to your suite immediately, miss."

"Can you send up some sweet tea too?" Mia asks with a smile.

"Of course, of course," he says, still flustered at having to deal with a major star being carried through his very posh lobby.

"Thank you so much. I really mean it. Thank you," she says as the elevator doors open and we step in.

"It's our pleasure, miss. We only want your visit with us to be the very best it can be."

I force a smile for him as the doors close because he looks like he's about to have a breakdown. I guess it isn't every day that one of their guests has something happen to them and shows up in a man's arms.

We silently ride up in the elevator, but right before we reach her floor, Mia quietly says, "I overreacted back at that bar. I'm sorry, Liam. Those people just wanted to see me."

Staring straight ahead at the gold doors reflecting the image of her in my arms back at us, I growl at the memory of what those people tried to do. "They were like animals. That's not wanting to see someone. That's wanting a piece of someone."

"Are you mad at me, Liam? You're acting like you are," she says, her words full of hurt.

I don't look down at her, but out of the corner of my eye I see her staring up at me like she desperately needs me not to be angry. I'm not angry with her. I'm angry with me. I fucked up. I let those animals get close to her because I dropped my guard.

I'm saved from having to answer her when the elevator rings to announce we've reached her suite and the doors open. Her crew is having a good time, but everything stops dead when they see me walk out of the elevator with Mia in my arms.

"Oh, my God! Mia, what happened?" her life coach asks in a voice that sounds remarkably similar to the frantic one the concierge guy had downstairs.

She rushes over to greet us as I set Mia down on the gold print sofa in the lounge area of the suite. "You're bleeding. Let me get you a washcloth to wipe it up. What happened? You said you were going out for a little bit. I figured you meant you were staying in the hotel, though, like always. If I had known you were going somewhere with whatever attacked you, I would have chained you to the floor."

Mia looks up at me and rolls her eyes. "Ainsley gets a little freaked at the sight of blood. Sit down. You can have some of my pizza. It should be here soon."

"No, that's okay. I need to get back downstairs to talk to my guys."

She reaches out her hand to grab mine and keep

me there, but I step back, needing to get out of this room full of all of these people gawking at her.

A look of hurt settles into her eyes. "What's wrong? Are you okay?"

I shrug, needing to get away from all of these people. Including Mia. "I'm fine. It looks like you're in good hands, so I'm going to go."

Before she can try to convince me to stay, I hurry over to the elevator, nearly running into one of the hotel's waiters coming out with Mia's pizza in his hands. Sidestepping him, I rush in as the doors close, quietly apologizing for nearly flattening him as he tried to make his delivery.

Regret fills me with every second that passes on my way down to my floor. I utterly failed in my job tonight. I can't forgive myself.

CHAPTER THIRTEEN

ia

ALL THE PEOPLE BUZZING AROUND ME TO MAKE sure I'm comfortable, happy, and fed only serve to make me wish Liam was still here. Why did he leave? He's angry, but I don't know why.

That's not true. I know him well enough to understand that tonight I broke one of his rules and now he's regretting going with me to that bar. I knew he was trying to keep us from going with all those reasons why we shouldn't even try to get into a bar, but I figured once we slept together everything changed.

Or is it that he's regretting that instead of what happened after we had sex?

God, I wish he was here. Everyone's attention seems fixed on me, and I feel like some freak at the circus. The blood on my shoulder was from a tiny scratch. Nothing big. I don't even think it was that much blood since I don't need a bandage or anything.

Liam's so overprotective. I love that about him, but he shouldn't be unhappy about what happened tonight.

Part of that is my fault. I overreacted when all those people started coming at me. I should be used to that. I've had people clamoring to get close to me for years. I had Liam there with me, the one person I trust more than any other in the entire world. If only I hadn't freaked out, everything would have been fine.

"So what happened?" Ainsley asks as Crystal sits down next to her to hear the story.

I wave away her question, not wanting to rehash my mistake. "Nothing happened. Liam and I were having a couple drinks at a bar and it got crowded. Things got a little crazy, but he got me out of there before anyone could hurt me."

"Was it the stalker?" Crystal asks in a voice full of fear.

"No. It was just a bunch of people out having a good time that got a little out of hand. Really, it wasn't a big deal. I think the scratch on my shoulder happened when someone fell into me and I caught my arm on a barstool. Seriously, you don't have to worry about me. Liam would never let anyone do anything to harm me."

Crystal lets out a heavy sigh, clearly relieved by what I'm saying, but Ainsley simply sits next to her shaking her head. I so don't need her ridiculous anger about the only man I can truly trust right now.

"What? Why are you sitting there giving me that look and shaking your head?" I snap, challenging her to give her opinion, even though I'm not in the mood for it.

I can see in her eyes she wants to tell me what's on her mind, but she merely shrugs, keeping her ideas about Liam to herself for once. "Nothing. I'm just scared after seeing him bring you in and the blood on your shoulder. You know how I get whenever I see blood. A nurse I could never be."

"Well, you don't have to be worried or scared or anything. Liam took care of everything, including me. Nobody touched me. Nothing bad happened. It just got a little edgy for a few minutes there. If anything, it was my fault for telling him I wanted to go to a bar tonight. I should have known there would be people there who might want to meet me."

Ainsley listens to all I have to say and then leans forward toward me. "But how did they know it was you? You were wearing the blond wig."

Suddenly, I realize I don't have it on anymore. I feel the top of my head and know that wig is long gone somewhere in that bar. Looking at Crystal, I reach my hand out to take hers.

"I am so sorry. In the ruckus, it must have slipped off. I'll replace it. I promise. I'm sorry, Crystal."

"Oh, sweetie, it's okay," she says, genuinely happy only her wig got lost in the shuffle. "I have lots of wigs, and I even have a few exactly like the one you were wearing. You don't have to replace it, but if you want, you can get me a nice long one. I've been thinking that's the next one I want to add to my collection. A nice long, platinum blond wig. I saw one a few weeks ago and it was so great! Wait until you see it!"

Ainsley sits back and folds her arms across her chest. "Well, that's all well and good, but shouldn't Liam have made sure no one could touch you at all? Isn't that his entire job?"

My emotions nearly boil over at hearing her attack him like that, and I swing my feet off the sofa to stand up because I need to get the hell away from her right now. She stares up at me in shock that I don't answer either of her asinine questions before I march into my bedroom and order everyone to leave.

"Time to go, guys! I need to get some rest. Feel free to hang out in the outer room, if you want."

I hear someone walking behind me, so I spin around to see who it is. Ainsley stops dead and levels her gaze on me, like she expects that I'll answer either of her questions now before I go to sleep.

"Whatever you're trying to say about Liam, you need to back off. He did exactly what I wanted him to do tonight. I wanted to go to a bar, so he accompanied me and made sure I was safe. It's not his fault some assholes got into a bar brawl and knocked into me. So I don't want to hear your opinion, Ainsley. Good night!"

She stands in the doorway wide-eyed and surprised I've shut down any chance for us to talk about this issue right now. I might not even talk about it tomorrow or ever, for that matter. Her opinion about him means nothing to me. Ainsley needs to learn if you don't have anything nice to say, don't say anything at all.

Her mouth opens like she wants to rebut all I've told her, but I slam the door before she can utter a single syllable. If she wants to talk tomorrow, that's fine, but if all she has to offer is more negativity about the man I'm crazy about, she can keep that to herself.

I close my eyes and fall back onto the bed, exhausted but thrilled about tonight. Liam and I slept together, and it was incredible! Now I just need to convince him nothing that happened at the bar was his fault. Knowing him, that will be easier said than done.

Then a thought occurs to me. Maybe it would be easiest sung.

Scrambling across the bed to look for my journal and pen I keep with me whenever I travel, I begin to jot down some ideas for a song that will let him know how much he means to me and how much none of tonight could be blamed on him. For the first time in a long time, my mind works faster than my pen, so I have to hurry to keep up with my thoughts. They come faster than I can keep up, though, so I begin to sing them in the hopes that I'll remember each one better.

I sing and write, and it all comes out quicker than I ever thought a song could come. The music practically writes itself, a song meant to be sung by me alone with only a piano on stage. I imagine the lights dimmed and only a single spot on me as I share my feelings for Liam with the entire world, but only he'll know I'm singing about us. Everyone else will think it's just another love song written by Mia.

By the time I finish nearly two hours later, I couldn't sleep if I wanted to. I have to get this song recorded. I can't wait to be sure the track is down so I can listen to it and see where it needs little tweaks.

It has to happen tonight.

Grabbing my phone, I call my mother to get her onto the task of having the plane ready for me. She answers in a groggy voice like I've woken her up out of a sound sleep. I look over at the clock and see it's barely midnight.

"I need to fly to Miami right now. Get the pilot and the plane ready. I'll leave as soon as I can get to the airport."

The response I get is silence from her end. Did she fall back to sleep, or is she simply in shock that I want to fly down to the recording studio I love the most to get this track down before dawn?

"Are you there? You heard what I said, right?" I ask, already irritated by her lack of enthusiasm.

She knows if I'm saying I want to go to Miami that I'm planning to record something. You'd think she'd be all for that. More songs to please the fans and bring more money in. She usually cares more about that than anything else.

"I heard you. I'm just not sure I understand. You want to fly to Miami tonight and do what?"

How is she not getting this? Inspiration has struck,

and I'm sitting here trying to explain the basics of what I want to do tonight. Some manager she is.

"I want to fly to Miami to get into the studio. I have a song that needs to be recorded right now. So get that pilot and my plane ready. It will be me and Liam. Maybe more, if he wants to have more of his guys with him. I'm going to leave everyone else here to enjoy themselves since we don't have another stop on the tour for three days in Houston. I'll be back tomorrow, so I won't miss a date."

That seems to make it through the fog of her sleepiness, and she perks up. "Okay, the pilot will need an hour or so, I'm sure. You know what he says about filing flight plans and all of that. Maybe two hours. Do you want me to come with you like always?"

The thought of my mother there as I sing my feelings for Liam instantly tarnishes what this song means to me, and I shake my head in horror, even if I answer her like it's nothing big that she can't be there. "No, not this time. With everyone else staying here, I need you to keep an eye on things."

"Okay. I can do that. Now when I have to tell the pilot how many of you will be traveling, what do I say?"

"At least two, but maybe three or four," I say as I shimmy across the bed to begin getting ready to go.

"Got it. Okay, I'll call him now. Give him two hours, but if it's longer, I'll let you know. And when will you be coming back? He'll want to know so he can file a flight plan for that trip too."

My mother almost sounds like she's trying to make

excuses for wanting to know my plans, something she never even attempts to apologize for. It's so totally her style to want to know the itinerary down to the minute. This attempt to respect my freedom feels like a change I will enjoy, if she keeps it up.

"I'd want to return tomorrow night. Liam will need to take his guys early to Houston to check everything out, so no later than tomorrow night by this time."

"Okay, Mia. I'm on it. I'm surprised you want to go into the recording studio so spur of the moment. You usually need time to gear up for a session. What changed?"

I hear her question and silently answer it for myself alone. Tonight changed me. Liam changed me. Having him in my life changed me.

Falling in love changed me.

But none of those answers are anything I want to share with her, so I casually answer, "Nothing much. Inspiration can hit at the strangest times, and I guess a suite at the Ritz-Carlton in New Orleans did the trick. I'll talk to you when I get back. Thanks for keeping an eye on things while I'm gone."

"Good luck with the new song. I can't wait to hear it!"

Transportation to Miami handled, next up is telling Liam he needs to be ready to leave in less than two hours. Hopefully, his mood has improved by now.

CHAPTER FOURTEEN

iam

FOR OVER AN HOUR AND A HALF, I'VE PACED BACK and forth across this hotel suite as my self-loathing has grown to fill every part of me. I should have never let Mia convince me to take her out to a bar tonight. What the fuck was I thinking?

I stop in front of the bed where only a few hours ago we lay naked in each other's arms and shake my head. Who am I kidding? She didn't have to convince me to do anything. I wanted to take her out because I knew it would make her happy.

That doesn't change the fact that I dropped the goddamned ball when it came to protecting her.

As I begin to pace again, thoughts of the two of us together in bed begin to crowd out my hatred for what I let happen tonight. I can't allow that. No matter how good it felt to be inside her, I don't deserve to enjoy those memories when the next thing that happened was a crowd of people nearly ripped her to shreds.

Someone knocking on my hotel room door tears me out of my thoughts, and I pad over to see who it is, hoping it won't be her. I can't face her tonight. Not after what happened.

I look through the peephole and see it's Mia smiling like she doesn't have a care in the world. Fuck. I thought she'd stay in her room until morning. I should have put one of the guys on each floor to make sure she didn't roam off.

Flinging open the door, I grab her by the arm and yank her into my room. Before I can slam the door shut, I snap, "What the hell are you doing just walking around the hotel all alone? You could get hurt, Mia."

She stares at me with a look of pure confusion and shakes her head. "I literally rode down one floor in the elevator from my room, got off in this hallway, and walked to this room. Since you guys and the rest of my entourage take up all the rooms on this floor, Liam, I think I'm safe to walk around on my own."

I slam the door and walk past her on the path I've paced for the past nearly two hours, avoiding meeting her gaze. "You take too many chances, you know that? I'm your head of security, and I can tell you when you do that, you don't make my job any easier."

"It's no big deal, Liam. Really. Why are you so upset?" she asks as I hear her walk up behind me.

Mia attempts to wrap her arms around my waist, but I turn out of her hold before she can and start my walk back across the room toward the door again. "It is a big deal. I need to know where you go at all times. I know you hate that, but it's the way it has to be. I thought you understood that."

"I do. You know I do. I haven't given you a hard time about how you protect me in weeks. Why are you so upset with me right now?"

Every word is filled with hurt, and I avoid meeting her gaze now because I can't see that in her eyes and know I put it there. "I'm not upset. I'm just trying to do my job the best I know how, Mia. I'm responsible for your safety. I can't forget that, even if I want to."

She doesn't say a word, and when I turn back to walk toward her, I can't avoid seeing how upset I'm making her. It's written all over her face, and just as I suspected, she's got tears in her eyes.

From me.

Finally, she asks in a tiny voice, "Why do you want to forget you're responsible for my safety? I thought that meant the world to you, Liam."

Christ, I should have just kept my mouth shut. I always get myself in trouble when I let myself talk too much. Now she thinks I don't care about being her bodyguard, a job that means more to me than she can ever imagine.

Facing her for the first time since she walked into my room, I try to find the right words so I don't make things worse. "That's not what I meant. Trust me. I don't want to forget anything when it comes to protecting you."

My answer makes her smile, but the corners of her lips barely rise. "Okay."

We stand there staring at one another like two strangers who don't know what to say next or two opposing armies that have little interest in continuing this battle. I don't want to fight with her. I'm too busy beating myself up to argue with the person I let down.

After nearly a minute, I ask, "So why are you roaming around the hotel after midnight? I figured you'd be sleeping by now after the night you had."

I don't go into detail about that, and I hope she thinks I'm referring to the show and not what happened afterward. Well, not the sex, which was great, but what happened after that.

Jesus. Now she's going to think I'm making some childish reference to our sleeping together. It would have been better if I didn't open the door at all.

"I need to fly out to Miami tonight to record a song. I know it's short notice, but when the muse comes, you don't ask her why she didn't wait for a more convenient time. So you need to get ready, and whoever else you want to join us needs to be ready in an hour. We'll leave right after one."

Her announcement stuns me. She wants to fly to Miami in the middle of the night to record a song? She can't wait until tomorrow?

"What do you mean? I need to take the guys to Houston ahead of the show there to make sure everything's set. I can't go to Miami tonight."

As I say those words, her expression falls, like she's just heard the worst news of her life. I want more than anything to spend every waking minute with her, and the sleeping minutes I'd love to spend with her in my arms together in bed. I just can't forgive myself for screwing up so badly at that bar tonight.

"I thought you'd want to be there since you're the one who's in charge of security, but if you need to go on ahead to Houston, then I guess I'll have to go with whoever you think you can trust. It's only a short overnight trip to Miami and back. I should be back within twenty-four hours," she says, trying to act like she isn't disappointed.

Damnit, I'm fucking everything up. I should just go with her. She's supposed to have her head of security with her when she goes anywhere like this.

I can't. Not tonight. My head is too full of guilt to be in the right place to protect her properly. She deserves better than I can offer right now.

"I'll get Kip and Brett to go with you. Then I can catch them up on any changes we make when we do the walk-through in Houston," I say flatly, hoping she can't see how much I'm blaming myself for before.

"Okay. Brett's the giant one who's even bigger than you? Is there a reason you're sending him?" she asks as she takes a step toward me and then stops.

She's close enough that I could stretch my arms out and pull her into me like I want to, but I don't move and instead answer, "It's always good to have someone his size around. Promise me you won't do anything but go to the recording studio and back to the airport while you're in Miami and then only go from the airport to the hotel here. And I need the number for the studio too."

With a smile, she nods her head and walks over to me, wrapping her arms around my waist like she wanted to do when she first got here. Looking up at me, she says, "I promise. No roaming around the countryside making things difficult for my bodyguards, and I'll text you the number the minute I get back to my room."

My entire body relaxes for the first time since I saw her get caught up in that fight at the bar hours ago. The simple feel of her against me makes me think I'm not the worst possible man in the world for her.

"Thank you. I'll let them know they need to get ready to go."

Neither of us makes a move so I can call Kip and Brett, though. Mia seems to want to hold on to me, and I can't think of any good reason to not let her.

"I'm fine, you know. Even that scratch on my shoulder that was bleeding before isn't. We didn't have any Band-Aids upstairs, but I didn't need one. So whatever you're thinking about that bar thing, don't. I wouldn't trade the time we got to spend drinking kamikazes for anything."

I look down into her sweet face and shake my head. "This is when you should be bitching me out for not doing my job. Don't let me off the hook so easily, Mia."

She slides her hands from around my waist and cradles my face. "You did your job, Liam. Nobody expects you to make sure nothing ever happens when

I'm out of my house. You saw a problem begin to happen and you handled it, exactly what you're supposed to do. Stop beating yourself up because I got flustered over nothing."

"What happened to that woman who balled me out the first day I met her? I'm thinking she should make an appearance right about now," I say with a chuckle.

"Well, she met this guy who showed her she was being a royal pain in the ass, and now she tries not to be that because of him."

"Cute."

Standing on her tiptoes, she kisses me softly and whispers against my lips, "It's the truth."

"I think since you're going to be away for the day I'll take the guys to Houston and get the walkthrough done tomorrow instead of the day after. That way we'll have one last day to do whatever we want before we head to the next show."

Mia turns her head to look over toward the bed and then turns back to face me, wiggling her eyebrows. "I've got an idea about how we should spend that time, so you and your guys handle your thing and I'll go record my song. I can't wait for you to hear it."

"Will you be singing it at the Houston show?" I ask, curious since I have no idea about how songs are written or how long they take to perfect for a live performance.

She thinks about it for a minute and nods. "Maybe. It only involves me singing and playing the piano, so theoretically, as long as I can get it down well enough for a show, I could do it then. Maybe the Kansas City show. But you'll hear it eventually. You can be sure of that."

I push her brown hair off her face and press a tiny kiss to her forehead. "Remember, you promised not to give the guys a hard time."

For that, I get a big smile. "They aren't you, but I'll go easy on them. Be ready when I get back. I'm already planning to spend hours in that bed over there with you."

"Thanks for the warning. I better hit the gym before you get back. I'm going to need to be in shape for our reunion," I say, secretly letting myself off the hook a little bit more with every time she makes me smile.

Mia's gaze drifts down my body and then back up to meet mine. "I'm not worried about you being in shape. From what I've seen, you're perfect. I, however, better take some vitamins for what I have planned. I'll see you tomorrow night by midnight."

She kisses me one more time and then pulls away from my hold. I watch her leave and wish it was already tomorrow night and we were together in my bed.

Now to inform Kip and Brett that they're making an unscheduled detour tonight. I didn't tell Mia, but Brett's the only man I trust to take my place. I respect Drew more than anyone else in the business, but pound for pound, it's Brett I'll always call to replace me.

CHAPTER FIFTEEN

*M*ia

MY RECORDING TIME AT MY FAVORITE STUDIO
turned out better than I expected. Rarely have I ever
gotten a song down in one take, but I swear it's like
this song formed somewhere deep in my heart and
knew it had to come out right now. At least it's done
and now I can play around with it to perfect each note
before I perform it the first time.

Poking my head into the control room, I smile at
Larry and Craig sitting at their mixing board.
Brothers, they're both big guys with long beards that
make them look like they should be living in a cabin
deep in the woods and not in a city like Miami. They
started their business years before I was born, but
they were the only people willing to give me studio

time when I was first coming up. My mother always said they agreed because I was a cute kid.

Since that day they finally said yes, I try to record all my songs here at their studio. My record company always presses for me to go to bigger ones in LA or other places around the world, but I never agree.

"You were on fire in there," Craig says with a big smile. "I don't think I've ever heard you sound like that. You find Jesus or something?"

"Something," I say with a chuckle. "Thanks so much for coming in here in the middle of the night for me, guys. I owe you big."

The two of them look at one another and shake their heads. "You don't owe us anything, baby. We've been on the Mia train since it pulled out of the station right here in Magic City," Larry says, opening his arms to invite me in for one of those big bear hugs he loves to give.

I walk into the control room and hug each of them, so thankful for how much they've helped me. "This is going to be my next number one, guys. You watch."

"That's the attitude you need. Seriously, though, you seem different from how you usually are. What's going on with you?"

Knowing Brett and Kip are out in the hallway waiting to escort me back to the plane, I can't take a chance on telling the brothers about Liam and me. So I bend down and whisper to them, "I can't say much, but let's just say this. Love has a way of changing a girl."

The two of them light up at my news, but I quickly

wave my hands to stop them from getting loud, just in case my bodyguards are listening. "But don't say anything, okay? It's really new, and I don't want anyone to know. Not yet, at least."

Always the one to put a fine point on things, Craig levels his gaze on me and says, "Then you better keep it from that manager of yours or the whole world is going to know chapter and verse about this new guy in three point five seconds."

"Isn't that the truth?" I say with a laugh. "You might be underestimating Andrea. I don't think it would take her that long."

"Well, enjoy yourself, baby," Larry says, grabbing my hand. "You deserve it. You've worked hard for a long time. Now you deserve some you time."

"Thanks, guys. I'll be back next week to see what I can do to get this just right. Until then, stay loose."

That's what they always say when I'm leaving. Stay loose. I guess it's some throwback to their hippie days. What it means to me is stay safe and be happy.

"Stay loose, baby!" they call after me as I walk out.

Brett stands guard just outside the door, so I breathe a sigh of relief that I didn't tell the brothers about Liam and me. Stony-faced, the enormous man stares down at me without a hint of a smile. He's definitely not like my favorite bodyguard.

"Time to go back to New Orleans," I say as I walk past him.

He doesn't respond, but the other guy Kip smiles as I make my way down the hallway toward the back door. I guess that's something, but I'm used to having someone to talk to around me. Liam always speaks. I've been thinking he didn't speak a lot, but now that I'm with these two, he's practically a chatterbox.

"Not a lot to say, huh?" I mumble as Kip opens the door for me.

I step outside into the hot south Florida early morning and look up at the blue sky without a cloud to be found. It's going to be a great day. Since it's barely seven a.m., I'm guessing we can make it back to the hotel by noon.

Then I remember I left my phone inside the studio. Spinning around, I point toward the door as my two bodyguards stare at me like they don't know what to do. "Forgot something. I'll be right back."

See, that's not like Liam either. He'd flat out ask me where I thought I was going. All this time, I thought he was pretty damn rude when he asked questions like that, but now that I hear nothing as I walk back into the building, I miss someone noticing what I'm up to.

On my way past the brothers' room, I explain, "I forgot my phone."

The two of them smile and nod, mostly because it's a very typical thing for me to do. I always seem to leave something behind.

I find it on the piano seat and hold it up for them to see through the window. "Got it! See you later!"

That gets me more nods and another smile from each of them. As I walk back toward the car, I stuff my phone into my purse and throw open the steel door to the gorgeous morning outside. I'm surprised not to see Liam's men, but I head toward the black SUV anyway. That's also not something my guy would do. I know he trusts these two implicitly, but is it standard procedure to just let a client roam around unprotected like this? He must have warned them about my tendency to want to go off on my own.

Then again, it is only a few yards to where the car is parked. I glance left and right to see no one around, so maybe I'm making a big deal out of nothing.

Liam really is wearing off on me. Next thing I know, I'll be quoting rules and regulations to everyone.

I reach out to open the backseat door, but the car's still locked. What's going on? Is this some strange bodyguard prank Brett and Kip are playing on me?

"Funny. You got me. Did Liam tell you to punk me?"

Silence.

I press my nose to the window and try to see in through the tinted glass. "Can you please open the door? You know, I'm not sure what you're doing, but Liam would never have me standing outside like this all alone."

Still, they say nothing. I try the door again, but it's still locked. What the fuck?

As I attempt to understand what the hell is happening, something hard hits me in the back of the head. I stumble forward into the car door, and then everything goes dark.

❧

"WAKE UP, PRINCESS. YOU CAN'T SLEEP ALL DAY."

I hear the voice telling me I need to wake up, but I don't understand. I struggle to open my eyes, and no matter how hard I try, I can't seem to get them to do as I want. It's like my brain isn't sending the right signal to get them to do the very thing they're being told to do.

"Open your eyes, Mia. Open your eyes!"

Now the voice, which I know is a male's, barks at me angrily. I want to tell him I'm trying my hardest, but I can't seem to speak either. What the hell is wrong with me? Did I catch some flu? Or tetanus? That's the thing that makes it impossible to close your mouth, isn't it?

No, that's lockjaw. Doesn't that come from tetanus, though?

I try to figure out the answer, finally deciding that the opposite occurs, and you can't open your mouth with lockjaw. Not that it matters because I don't think the reason I can't get my damn mouth to work is because of that or tetanus.

"Jesus Christ, Mia! Open your fucking eyes!" the man yells again, this time directly in front of my face.

Wait a second. I know that voice. Who is screaming at me?

Finally, I manage to open my right eye enough to see the person in front of me, and instantly, I begin to shake my head. No way should he be standing in front of me yelling a single word in my face. What the fuck is Michael doing in my hotel room screaming at me to open my eyes?

"That's one. Do the second one and you'll get a treat," he says and then laughs.

I work to open my left eye, sure I've never used whatever muscle that is like this before in my entire life. It's like there's a five pound weight attached to my eyelid, but I finally get both eyes open to see Michael sitting in a chair in front of me in a place that is definitely not my hotel room or any room I've ever been in before.

"Attagirl. Now which do you want, orange juice or apple juice?" he asks in a snide tone, like I'm some imbecile he's charged with making comfortable.

My mouth drops open, but at first, no sound comes out. Too bad because I want to tell him to fuck off in the worst way. I've got a splitting headache that's suddenly making the back of my head pound like a kick drum, and I feel sick to my stomach, as if I haven't had enough food in me for far too long.

"Use your words, Mia. You know I can't give you what you want if you don't use your words."

God, he sounds like some asshole step-parent who thinks that's the way you talk to a child. But I'm not a child, and he's definitely not any parent of mine, step or otherwise.

I try to wet my lips, but my tongue is like a giant cotton ball. It takes me a few seconds to get enough saliva, and finally, I can say something to this jackass. "Fuck off. Where the hell am I?"

He grins like any of this is funny, and I slowly turn my head left and right to look around. Is this where he works now? It looks like a factory with cement walls and floors.

Then I look down at my body and see my hands and legs tied to a chair that reminds me of the ones we used to have in our dining room when I was a little girl. I try to move my right hand, but it's securely tied to the arm of this old wooden chair.

"Don't try to move. You're tied there, so if you try too hard, you might fall over and hit your head. We wouldn't want you to hurt yourself," he says as he stares at me like he's enjoying this.

"Where am I?" I snap, getting angrier by the minute.

"Somewhere safe. Now which do you want, orange or apple juice?"

"Fuck off and I don't want anything from you! Where are the two guards who were with me? What did you do to them?"

Michael shrugs. "Their services weren't needed any more, so I relieved them of their duties. If they didn't bleed out, they're probably reporting back to your new head of security that they lost their client. I imagine he's going to be more than a little pissed since you and he are an item now."

The thought of Brett and Kip hurt makes my chest hurt. "What did you do to them, Michael?" I sob.

"I needed them out of the way, so I shot them. For what it's worth, I didn't aim for their heads or any major organs. I just needed them indisposed. Assuming someone found them and took them to the hospital, they'll be fine after some orthoscopic surgery.

The knee is a tricky thing, Mia. You know that. Remember when you hyperextended yours a few years ago when you were rehearsing a new routine? We almost had to reschedule that tour because of that little mishap."

I hate the way he talks like he had anything to do with my business. He was the man in charge of keeping me safe for far too long, and he didn't even do that job well, but he sure as hell didn't have a say in whether that tour would be rescheduled or not.

"*We* didn't almost have to do anything. *I* had to make that decision. You never had any part in that." I practically spit out the words as I continue to attempt to get these ropes around my wrist loose.

"Don't bet on it, princess," he says, sneering like he knows so much more than I do about everything. "I've been in on everything that happened with you for years."

"What are you talking about? You're suffering from delusions of grandeur, Michael. You were the guy who oversaw my security, poorly, I now know, and you were the person I turned to because I thought you were my friend. Come to find out you were a piss-poor version of that too."

He jumps up out of his chair and lunges at me, sticking his face directly in front of mine as he presses his palms down on my shoulders. The weight makes my body instantly hurt all over and all I want to do is cry. I won't let him see me give in like that, though.

"I did everything exactly as you wanted me to. Everything, you bitch! You didn't want to feel like you were trapped in your own house, so I made sure you didn't feel that way. You didn't want to have to feel like your security took away from your precious, little life, so it never did. You were the reason you weren't safe, not anyone else!"

Turning away so I don't have to look at his ugly features anymore, I say, "I didn't know any better. You did. You're a grown man who is supposed to know how to protect a client."

Finally, he leans away from me, removing his hands from my shoulders, so I turn back to face him and add, "If more had to be done, then it should have been."

He smiles as he backs up toward his chair, but it's not a smile of sweetness or happiness. "Oh, you have the answers for everything."

I say nothing, unsure if his anger will escalate if I do. My mind races with questions about how long I've been here, if anyone knows I'm missing, and if anyone is looking for me.

Most of all, will Liam find me in time to save me from this madman?

"As for my being your friend, you knew I wanted more. You wanted it too, you little cock tease. I never knew how much until you showed up at my door that day and saw me with Tracey. Didn't like seeing me like that, did you? Poor little Mia missed her chance. You should have taken me up on my offers all those times."

His cruelty comes through loud and clear in every word, but I can't stop myself from setting him straight. "I never wanted you. That's not how I ever saw you. I thought you were my friend. So much for that, I guess."

Rage flashes in his eyes, and he barks, "I didn't want to be your fucking friend! I never wanted to be put into that box, and you knew that, you fucking tease!"

"What exactly do you think you're doing with this whole thing here? Are you planning on asking for a ransom for me? You'll never get away with this, Michael."

Instead of enraging him further, that makes him smile. "Oh, don't worry. I'm not alone in this, so I'll get away with anything I do. You can choose to behave yourself, or you can choose to get hurt. It's entirely up to you."

Never once in all the times I turned to this man for all those years did I think he could ever hurt me. Now I truly don't know for sure.

All I know is I've never needed Liam more. Where is he? Is he coming to take me out of this place?

"And if you're thinking where is your new head of security when you need him most, my partner has taken care of that. Settle in, sweetheart. You're here for the duration."

Michael walks away, leaving me sitting in that chair and more terrified than ever. His partner has taken care of Liam? What does he mean?

An ache settles into my chest at the thought that Liam's been hurt. Or worse, he's dead at the hands of Michael's partner, whoever he is.

CHAPTER SIXTEEN

iam

I WAKE TO THE SOUND OF MY PHONE RINGING AND grab it off the nightstand to see it's right after eight in the morning. So much for sleeping in a little today. My eyes focus a little bit more so I can see it's Andrea calling.

Not the person I ever want to wake up to.

After scrubbing my face of the last vestiges of sleep, I answer the call. "What's up, Andrea?"

"Mia's been taken! Those two men you sent with her to protect her didn't do their job, and now she's God only knows where!"

She begins to cry hysterically while I sit upright in bed and immediately launch into work mode. My mind's racing with questions about where Mia could be, who could have done this, and where the hell Brett and Kip are in this whole thing.

"Tell me everything you know. I need to know every detail right now," I say as I swing my legs out of bed.

From the second my feet hit the floor, I'm running one hundred percent on adrenaline. The woman I've fallen in love with is missing and who knows where, and two of my men are unaccounted for. None of this is good. Every minute I waste waiting for Andrea to get her shit together and stop crying is a minute any of them may be hurt.

Or worse.

She continues to sob as she tries to tell me what she knows, but I can't understand a goddamned word of it. "Andrea, calm down. I need to be able to figure out how to go from here, but I can't find out where here is if you keep crying."

I listen to her slowly stop her wailing, and then she sniffles a few times before saying, "I got a call about ten minutes ago. It was someone saying they took Mia. They want a ransom for her."

So it's a kidnapping. That she waited ten minutes to tell me about. Okay, focus, Liam. That means they want something in exchange for Mia, so they're going to keep her alive.

At least until they get paid.

"How much do they want?" I ask as I yank my pants up my legs.

"What?"

"How much is the ransom?" I ask again while I

button my pants and walk over to the closet to find a shirt.

"I don't know. I mean, I can't remember," Andrea says.

What the fuck does she mean she can't remember?

Ripping my grey dress shirt off the hanger, I try to find the patience to deal with this woman right now. "Okay, let's go over what happened, step-by-step. What did they say?"

"They said they have her and they want five million. That's it. That's how much they said they want. I guess in all of this I just forgot. They want five million dollars for her."

"Okay," I say as I let out a sigh, happy to be getting somewhere with her finally. "When do they want it by?"

"Today!" she squeals, like I should have known that answer without even asking the question. "They want it today or they're going to kill her. We have to get it to them immediately!"

"I agree, but they don't want to kill her, Andrea. Trust me. This is for money. Kidnappers rarely want to be murderers. They want money so they can go live the life they want to live. Being charged with a capital crime in the state of Florida is not what they got into this for, so they're going to keep her alive."

At least I hope so.

"Did they say where they want us to drop off the money? How is it to go down?" I ask as I finish putting my shoes on.

"No. They didn't say anything about that. Oh,

God! Does that mean they're going to kill her because I didn't have the money to offer right then and there?" Andrea asks, sobbing again.

"No, no. Calm down. They said they'd call back, right? They want money, so they'll give us details about how to get them the money in the next call. Did they say anything else?"

"Yes. They said not to call the police or the FBI. I wasn't going to, Liam, because they never do anything. I swear they want to wait until she gets hurt until they do something. Oh, my God! Is this her stalker? Has he graduated to kidnapper now?"

That already occurred to me, but I quickly dismissed that idea. Just as kidnappers rarely want to become murderers, stalkers rarely make the leap to kidnappers. It's an entirely different focus and unlikely one a stalker would want to get involved with.

"No, I don't think this is her stalker, so let's not get worried about that. We do have to contact the FBI, at least, though. This is a kidnapping, and as much as we might want to think we can handle things ourselves, the FBI knows how to deal with this better than anyone else in the world."

"Mia won't like that, Liam. She never wants to deal with the police or FBI. She doesn't think they ever want to help. That's why she leaves dealing with them to me, but I have to admit, I think she's right. I doubt they'll even take this seriously since she's only been gone for about eight hours."

I grab my suit jacket and head toward the door. "We're contacting the FBI, Andrea. Not to contact them will risk Mia's life, and we don't want that. I can be the one who deals with them. I've done it before, so it's no problem. As soon as I finish this call with you, I'll get in touch with them."

"No, no. I can't have you do that. They'll only end up wanting to talk to me because I'm her mother. I'll do it."

Confused, I say, "Mia's not a minor anymore, Andrea. You don't have to be the point person on this. I can do it. In fact, I should since two of my guys were with her and I need to find out where the hell they are."

"That's even more reason for me to handle the FBI. I'll take care of them, Liam. Just be ready when they get here because they'll need to know all the details about when Mia left. I don't know because I was sleeping. You deal with finding your men. God, I hope they aren't…"

She doesn't finish her sentence before she begins crying again. I don't need to hear the rest of what she was thinking. I've already said those exact words to myself.

God, I hope they aren't dead.

DREW ANSWERS HIS HOTEL ROOM DOOR IN A PAIR OF shorts and a T-shirt that says Auburn on it. I don't know why I notice that, but as he steps back to let me in, I ask, "Is that where you went to college?"

Confused, he shakes his head. "No. Why are you here early asking me about my shirt?"

"Mia's mother got a call from kidnappers a half hour ago. They have Mia and they want five million for her. I don't know where Brett and Kip are, but I've checked with the pilot and they never came back to the plane."

"Jesus Christ, man. Where the hell did they go and why weren't you with them?"

I shake my head, hating myself right now. "Long story. Mia decided she needed to fly out to Miami to the recording studio and I felt like I should stay here to do the walk-through in Houston today. So I sent Brett and Kip to guard her. There's no way they'd let anyone take her if they had the ability to stop them."

My friend knows what I'm trying not to say out loud.

Holding his hand up, he says, "Stop right there. I know what you're thinking, but it's not a sure thing. Kidnappers rarely like to kill people. They're in it for the money. Nothing else."

His attempt at making me think logically makes me chuckle. "Yeah, I just told Andrea that."

"So don't go thinking Brett and Kip are done for yet. You said you contacted the pilot and he hasn't seen them. Did you contact the recording studio?"

I whip out my phone as I shake my head. "Fuck, why the hell am I not thinking clearly? That's why I came to you. My head is a fucking mess right now, Drew."

"Call there and see if you can find out anything. I'm going to get dressed and get the rest of the guys ready for when we head out."

Drew leaves me alone, and suddenly, I feel like nothing is going to be okay. I should have never assigned them the job of guarding her on this goddamned spur of the moment trip to Miami. That was my responsibility, but after fucking up things at that bar, I didn't think I should be the one to go with her.

Goddamnit! This is my fault.

The phone at the recording studio rings for what seems like five minutes before someone finally answers the call. Some guy named Larry tells me Mia left right before seven, more than an hour ago. He says she left with the two bodyguards she had with her and he and his brother haven't heard anything since they walked out with her.

"I need you to check outside. Mia's missing, as are my two guys. There should be a rental car there. A black SUV," I say, my heart racing at the good news he's just told me.

They've only been gone for a short time. That's good. At least I hope it is.

"Okay. Hang on. I'll check."

Pacing back and forth across Drew's hotel room, I listen for any indication this Larry person found Brett and Kip, but I hear nothing. When he returns less than a minute later, he only has bad news.

"I checked, and the SUV is still here. The doors are locked, but I looked in and saw no one. I think I saw something red that looked like blood a couple yards away, though."

Fuck. Blood means someone's hurt.

"Okay, I need you to call the police. Tell them we've got the FBI on it here, but three people are missing down there and at least one is likely in need of medical attention. Have them call me at this number and coordinate with us here."

After I finish the call, I throw my phone across the room, furious that I let this happen to Mia and my guys. What kind of fucking chief of security am I if I can't keep the one person I'm supposed to keep safe from being taken right off the goddamned street?

Drew walks back in and picks up my phone where it landed after it hit the wall. "Chill out, man. You need to keep your head right now. You care about her and the guys, so keep things level, all right?"

Nodding, I stuff my phone into my pants pocket and let out a deep sigh. "I should have been there with her. I'll never forgive myself if all three of them don't come back safe and sound when this is all over."

"They will. Nothing's certain yet, so let's think positive. Have the FBI been called in?"

"Yeah, Andrea is handling that. I need to find Brett and Kip. I think we need to head down to Miami. Not that I don't think the cops can handle things, but I'd feel better if we were closer to the scene."

Drew grabs his jacket off the back of the chair next to the window. "I agree. When do we leave?"

As we walk out into the hallway heading toward Jack's room, I quickly try to find the best way to get there. It has to be by plane. We could drive, but that would take too long, and even if we have to wait a few hours to get a flight, flying will still take less time.

"You get ready and get Jack in on all of this. I'll get us a flight out as soon as I can this morning. Make sure you bring him up to speed on all that's happened."

I stop to reserve us three tickets, and Drew gives me a reassuring pat on the back. "Stay positive, man. Nothing's bad until we learn it's bad. Until then, it's all good. Don't forget that."

"Yeah, you're right. Thanks, Drew."

Left alone in that hotel hallway, I try to convince myself he's right, that we've heard nothing bad yet, so we shouldn't worry. But I can't stop myself from picturing Mia being held hostage in some terrible place with people who don't see her as anything but a way to get millions of dollars.

Even worse is the thought that two of my guys I brought onto this job could be lying hurt somewhere bleeding out or worse.

Fuck, I can't think like that! I need to get my shit in gear and be the man Mia and my guys need me to be right now. That means buying plane tickets and getting the fuck down to Miami to find them. Self-loathing can wait until after we save them from the assholes who thought it was a good idea to kidnap Mia.

CHAPTER SEVENTEEN

 ia

My wrists feel raw after all these hours of trying to escape from these ropes. Fucking Michael! I swear to God if I get out of this alive, I'm going to make sure he pays for this.

I can't think that way. Not if I get out of this alive. No, Liam would never let this asshole kill me. No way. I don't know how, but he'll find a way to rescue me and make this shithead pay dearly for taking me.

Desperate to find some way out of here, I scan the room to see if there's anyone here other than Michael and me. I haven't seen anyone yet, but someone could be hiding out in another part of the building. I need to figure out a way to get out of these restraints. Even if I don't know where I am, if I could run, I know I could escape.

"Always fighting reality. You know, if you'd just go with the flow, you wouldn't have ended up in this mess in the first place."

I see Michael walking toward me wearing that smug look he's had on his face nearly the whole time he's kept me here. Why does he think he's going to get away with this? He must be insane.

"It's not reality. This isn't reality," I say, trying to egg him on to explain what the hell all of this is about. "Kidnapping people isn't normal, you know."

Rolling his eyes, he shrugs like this is all in a day's work for him. "Famous people get kidnapped all the time. It doesn't make the news because they pay off the kidnappers and keep the whole thing hush-hush, but it happens a lot."

"People are going to miss me. I'm not sure how you think this is going to work. I've got hundreds of people on my staff between my entourage, my security, and my management team, not to mention everyone on my tour crew needing me to make it to Houston in just a couple days to perform. You don't think they've contacted the authorities to search for me?"

He shakes his head and grins. "No, I don't."

"Are you joking? My mother will be up one side of the police and down the other when she finds out I'm gone, and you can trust me, she already knows. I have no idea how long you've kept me here, but you can be damn sure the moment she found out, she made sure to call everyone up to the President himself to get me back."

There are few things about my mother that I truly appreciate, but her desire to make sure I'm safe and sound at all times is one of them. Most times, that trait of hers is nothing but oppressive, but at moments like this, I'm sure it's coming in handy.

When Michael doesn't respond, I know I've touched a nerve with my mention of my mother. "You may have convinced her that she should give you another chance to work for us, but you know her. Once she fires someone, she's done with them. I'm guessing you told her some sad story to make her hire you back, but Andrea Shanoff isn't someone you should rely on for tender feelings. I learned that years ago. I would have thought you'd understood that too after being around us for so long."

He laughs and walks behind me, sending chills down my spine when he wraps his hands around my throat. Leaning down, he whispers in my ear, "That mother of yours sure does have a way of being vindictive, doesn't she? She knew full well that I only got you that hotel room because you asked me to, and still she fired my ass. Andrea absolutely understands what it takes to be in the music business. She's got ice water in her veins. Odd that you didn't have any of that rub off on you."

I turn to look at him, hating how close his face is to mine. How could I have ever entertained the idea of Michael as anything to me even for a fleeting moment? His face is nothing but ugly to me now. The mouth I used to love to see smile appears merely like a nasty slit, and the dark eyes that I thought showed how much he cared whenever he looked at me are just empty as they stare at me in hatred.

For a moment, I want to cry at how wrong I was about him, but I harden myself to keep from falling apart. He needs to see the steely determination in my eyes. I'm not some wilting flower he has total control over. He may have my hands and feet bound to this damn chair, but he doesn't possess the power to stop me from thinking.

Michael seems to want to hear me talk, so he's going to get an earful.

"You think I don't have ice water in my veins. You have no idea who I am. I've fired people for practically nothing. I've risen to the heights I've reached in this business not only because I have talent but because I don't let anyone put me down. So whatever fantasy you have about Mia being a tender soul who wouldn't hurt a fly can just go fuck itself because that's never been who I am."

Michael throws his head back in laughter and comes around the chair to crouch down in front of me. I so wish I could wipe that arrogant ass smile right off his ugly face. Or better yet, I'd love to kick it off. If only I could get my hands and feet free of these ropes.

When he sets his palms on my knees, I stiffen, repulsed by the mere touch of his hands on my body. He enjoys how uncomfortable he's making me and lets out a low chuckle.

"So riddle me this, oh queen of ice water in her veins, how is it if you're such a cold-hearted bitch, why haven't you ever fired your mother from being your manager?" he asks in a mocking tone, all the while staring up at me with a knowing look I don't understand.

"Why would I fire my mother? She's a great manager," I say, wishing I didn't sound so half-hearted in my defense of my mother.

Our relationship is complicated, and I don't give a damn what this asshole thinks he knows about my mother and me. We've been through hard times that would have crushed other people. She was there for every rejection I got and every door that closed in our faces when I was first starting out. Yes, she drives me crazy, but she's my mother and I wouldn't be where I am today without her.

No matter how much I say I want to be in this business without her, I can't imagine singing another song or appearing on another stage without my mother as my manager. So whatever this jackass thinks he knows about Andrea and Mia Shanoff, he doesn't know squat.

"You complained to me every day I worked for you that she was anything but a good manager, nevermind great. It was nonstop. 'My mother makes my life a living hell. My mother won't let up.' Every day you bashed her, yet she's always employee number one in the Mia Enterprises world. Ask yourself why you practically despise her, but you won't fire her."

I shake my head, hating how he makes what I feel about my mother sound. "I don't hate her. You don't understand the relationship between mother and daughter. If you were a daughter, you'd know that no matter how much I complain, she's still my mother. She was the one person who stuck around when things weren't great, always believing that someday they would get better. Loyalty like that isn't the kind of thing someone forgets easily. We fight. I admit that. But she's my mother, and I love her."

Michael slowly slides his hands up my thighs as he asks, "Do you think she loves you?"

I twist my body in a desperate attempt to make him stop touching me. "Fuck you! I don't have to think about how to answer that. Of course, she loves me. She's my mother. She gave up everything so I could be where I am today. She shows her love every day, unlike other people who claimed to care but obviously didn't give a damn about me. And get your hands off me!"

He doesn't stop, though, and when he reaches the spot where my legs meet my body, I shake my head, not believing he'll do what I'm terrified he's about to do. Michael is a lot of things, but a rapist? I can't believe that.

"I cared, Mia. I cared and waited day after day for you to see I was the one who actually loved you more than anyone else, including Andrea. You never did, though, so at some point, I came to the realization that I needed to face the facts. You were fine with hanging out in my room and talking every night as you forced me to watch those stupid old TV shows you like. You loved having me at your beck and call, but you were never going to let me in like I wanted to. So I found a way to get some benefit from having to be around you after all."

I lower my head as tears fill my eyes. "I never led you on, Michael. Don't do this. You don't want to do this."

He digs his thumbs into the very tops of my legs and laughs, frightening me. "Do what? Fuck you? Right here? Don't be ridiculous! You aren't that good looking, and as you well know, I already have someone I can get it from whenever the hell I want. Jesus, Mia! You really are full of yourself."

"Stop it! You're hurting me," I sob, but it only makes him push into my flesh harder.

"Maybe you should have been nicer to me, Mia. Maybe you should have been the kind of woman who knew a good thing when she had it in front of her. But no, you're not that smart. Dumb bitch!"

Finally, Michael releases his hold on my legs, and I feel blood rush to the spots where his thumbs pressed down on my skin. I don't understand any of this he's doing. I didn't believe he was someone who would take a woman against her will, but then he acted like that's what was about to happen.

Now he's talking about how I wasn't nice to him and how stupid I am.

What is this about?

CHAPTER EIGHTEEN

iam

DREW, JACK, AND I STAY IN MY HOTEL ROOM, THE two of them sitting on the bed while I pace back and forth waiting to get someone from the Miami police to talk to me. I've gotten transferred to three different divisions on this one call, and I'm about to lose my fucking cool.

"What's so goddamned hard about telling me where they are?" I snap as I pass the bed heading toward the window.

"Maybe they don't know?" Jack suggests.

I want to blow up and ask how the fuck they couldn't know that two men have been fucking attacked, with at least one of them shot in their city, but that's stupid. Miami's a big place, so maybe they don't know.

But somebody has to fucking know something.

"Try to keep your calm, man. We don't know anything yet, so it all could be fine," Drew says in his attempt to be supportive.

I understand what he's trying to do. It's just that at this very moment, I want to beat the hell out of someone and I'm trying hard not to start a fight with either of the guys I know are worried just like I am.

Holding out of the phone toward them, I growl, "It's hard to stay calm when people keep putting you on fucking hold. I swear to God I'm going to explode on the next person who does."

Another two passes across the room and back and finally someone comes back onto the call. "Mr. Jackson, I'm Sandra Curry, chief of the fourteen precinct. I tracked down your men. They're at Jackson Memorial, ironically enough. One man, Brett Marshall, suffered a shot to his calf. The ER is handling him right now. The other man, a Trevor Jones, suffered a more severe injury with the gunshot shattering his kneecap. He's in surgery right now."

"Do you have any idea who did this? Because they were guarding a client and she's been kidnapped, I'm guessing by the same people who shot my men. Has the FBI coordinated with you there yet? She's been gone for over five hours."

My words are met with silence for so long that I pull the phone away from my ear to check if I somehow lost Chief Curry. I see the call is still live, so I say, "Is there something wrong?"

Still, she remains silent until she finally says, "Mr.

Jackson, we have no information on any kidnapping or any involvement of the FBI in any kidnapping of a woman here in Miami this morning."

Panic swirls in my mind, almost immediately replaced by pure anger. Andrea didn't call the cops or the FBI? Why? She doesn't think we can ride in on our white horses and find Mia all by our fucking selves, does she?

"Thank you, Chief Curry. The two men who were injured were guarding Mia, the singer. She was last seen at Hampton Roads Recording Studio this morning right around seven. We have no idea where she is or who took her or why. I'd been led to believe you and the FBI had been notified of her disappearance, but I see that isn't the case. I have to go handle this, but my men and I will be coming to Miami to hopefully find out who took her and see her home safe."

The chief says something about being sorry and offers her office's help in finding Mia, but I hear very little of it before I end the call and turn toward the door. As I storm past Drew and Jack, I bark, "Fucking Andrea never called the FBI or the cops. What the hell is wrong with this woman?"

I'm practically blind with rage as I run down the hallway to Andrea's room. Pounding my fist against her hotel room door, I yell, "Andrea, open this goddamned door so I can talk to you!"

She answers a few seconds later looking shocked I'm so angry. I push past her, barely able to focus I'm so furious right now. Inside her room, I see she's got what looks like an entire new wardrobe laid out on her bed, complete with sales tags still on the clothes.

"Did a little shopping this morning?" I snap, unsure what the hell I'm looking at.

"Well, yes," she says as she closes the door. "I've been waiting for the FBI and realized I didn't have anything to wear for when they meet with us, so I decided to get some new things. You don't understand how important it is when you appear on camera to look good. Men always look good because you get to wear a suit, but women have to choose an entire outfit."

I march over to her so we're face to face and shake my head, trying so damn hard not to lose my cool on this woman. "I know about you not contacting the FBI or the Miami police. I don't know what you're up to, Andrea, but your daughter's life is in danger and we can't be fucking around like this. Why didn't you call them?"

Sheepishly, she looks away to avoid my demanding gaze. "Mia wouldn't want that. I know I said I'd call like you told me to, but I know my daughter. She won't be happy when she finds out the police and the FBI got involved. We can handle this on our own. The kidnappers already told me where to bring the five million, and I'm in the process of waiting for the bank to send over the money right now. It's okay, Liam. Everything's going to be okay."

The top of my head feels like it's about to blow off, sending my brains all over this hotel room. My thoughts whirl from one terrible thing to another. It's going to be okay? How the hell does she figure that? Her daughter is missing, kidnapped by people who blew a hole in one of my guy's calf and a hole through another one of my guy's kneecap. What makes her think they won't hurt Mia once they get the money?

"I don't know what the hell you're thinking, but your daughter is in very real danger. I know I told you kidnappers don't usually turn to murderers, but that doesn't mean it never happens. The kidnappers clearly have guns. They shot two of my goddamned guys! One is going to be lucky if he ever walks right again, and although I'm not sure, it's highly unlikely he's going to able to work in my business ever again. Nothing is fucking okay, Andrea!"

Still she doesn't seem worried.

With a gentle pat to my forearm, she says with a smile, "Mia is going to be fine. You'd be surprised at how wonderful this is for PR. I've already contacted her agent, and she's getting the word out to the press right now. That's another reason why I needed new clothes."

Shaking my head in disbelief, I wonder if I'm losing my mind. "Are you honestly talking about how to capitalize on your daughter's kidnapping?"

Andrea nods and walks over toward the bed where all her new clothes lay to lift up a dark green dress. "In this business, you have to take advantage of anything you can, honey. The reviews for her Tampa concerts weren't fantastic, I'm sad to say. That one reviewer questioned whether Mia still has it. Can you believe that nonsense? Still has it? Screw her! Mia had that audience in the palm of her hand. Last night's show was one of the best she's ever put on, and there's no way I'm going to let some two-bit music writer from a Tampa newspaper drag down Mia's tour. Not if I have anything to say about it."

None of what she's saying makes sense. Maybe she's just compartmentalizing her fear over Mia having been kidnapped. Or maybe she's having some kind of psychotic break. I can't be sure.

All I know is every second I spend trying to figure out what the hell is wrong with her, the woman I love is in danger. She can fret about PR and reviewers' stupid comments about whether or not Mia still has it, but I need to find out what the fuck is going on and rescue her.

I turn to walk out of Andrea's room and say, "I've already reported Mia missing to the Miami police, and I'm going to call the FBI right now to make sure they're coordinating with the authorities down there."

Her response is silence, but then right before I reach the door, she says, "They aren't going to take her disappearance seriously. They never do."

Furious, I spin around and point at her bed full of new clothes. "Maybe if you spent more time being worried about your daughter and less time trying to find the perfect promotional angle when she's in danger, they would."

Then it suddenly dawns on me, hitting me like a bolt of lightning out of the blue. Andrea isn't worried about Mia now because she knows far more than she's telling me.

"What's going on here, Andrea? I'm done playing fucking games with you! Tell me!" I yell, making her jump at the bellowing sound of my voice bouncing off the walls of her hotel room.

Her eyes wide in fear now, she shakes her head, refusing to say anything. I'm not leaving this room until she explains exactly what she knows. I swear to God if I need to shake it out of her, I will.

"I'm not playing around with you and this nonsense anymore," I threaten as I march over to her. "Tell me what's going on. Now!"

Once again, the boom of my voice makes her jump. Taking a step back away from me, she rolls her eyes and says in frustration, "Fine. She's not really in danger, okay?"

My mouth drops open in shock at what she's just told me. "What do you mean she's not in danger? My two guys who were guarding her were really in danger. Kip might never walk again if that bullet tore through God only knows what in his knee. Brett took a bullet to his calf. That's real fucking danger, Andrea, so tell me what you mean."

"He wasn't supposed to hurt them seriously. I'm sorry about your guy's knee. That wasn't supposed to happen. I told him if he had to use the gun, to make it that the bullet went through some fleshy part like the upper arm or the thigh."

"The thigh?" I say, thankful neither Brett nor Kip got hit there. "You mean where the femoral artery is? The artery that if you hit it, you fucking bleed to death before anyone can goddamned help you? What is wrong with you? No wonder your daughter thinks you're a monster. You are!"

Good God. The kidnapper holding Mia thinks shooting someone in the thigh is a harmless flesh wound because of this woman. If he does that, there's no chance I'll be able to save her.

"I promise we'll pay for any medical bills and rehab costs both of your guys have. They'll get the best care in the world. You don't have to worry about that. We'll make sure the one who got shot in the knee is up and walking and doing whatever job he wants for the rest of his life. I promise, Liam."

Unable to control my anger, I grab her by the shoulders and squeeze my fingertips into them, needing her to feel something about what she's done. "You put three people in danger for what? So Mia could be on the news as some sympathetic creature and reviewers would say nice things about her concerts? What the fuck is wrong with you?"

Unlike her daughter, Andrea doesn't buckle under my interrogation of her and pushes against my chest to walk away from me. "I do what I have to so Mia can have all the success she deserves. Sometimes that means doing things that some people might not approve of, but you don't understand this business. If you aren't constantly in the spotlight, people forget about you. It's a savage world out there. I make sure everyone always has Mia's name on their lips. She doesn't know what I do, but if she did, she'd understand. She knows what this business is like. You better get used to it if you think you want to be with her too, or you'll get swept away like everyone else she's ever fallen for. Mark my words, Liam, you need to understand what it takes to be the man Mia's with or you won't last for long."

So she knew about us? She knew Mia and I were together and still pulled this stunt?

Grabbing her by the arm, I spin Andrea around to face me. "You fucked with the wrong man this time. No wonder the authorities don't take what happens to Mia seriously. They must know it's always you pulling some PR stunt."

"I never call them, so it's not like they could possibly get in the way. They wouldn't do anything anyway, not until she's hurt, at least. Don't you watch the news?" she asks in a smug voice that tells me she doesn't understand the harm she's caused.

"I'm done listening to this madness. Tell me where she is so I can go get her. And you better pray to God that she's not hurt or I swear, Andrea, I'll make sure you pay every way I can."

She waves off my threat and my worry, smiling up at me. "She's fine. Michael would never hurt her. Trust me."

I stagger back, confused at hearing that name again. "Michael? What is it with you two? First you bring him back to handle security, and now you're working with him to kidnap your daughter? What the fuck is going on with you and that guy?"

"That guy is the one who's helped me manage Mia for years, Liam."

My mind whirls with questions, and then one

jumps out over all the rest. "Were you planning to have him kidnap her after the show in Tampa? Is that why you brought him back and tried to push my guys out that night?"

Andrea's eyes open wide, as if she's horrified that I could accuse her of such a thing. "Don't be ridiculous! He was there because I needed him to be."

"Why? Why the hell did some guy who was shit at his job of protecting Mia suddenly need to be her security head again? You were planning this the whole time."

"She was never going to be hurt. He would never hurt her, and neither would I. You don't understand. The world Mia and I live in is different than the outside world. That bad review of her Tampa show could start a domino effect with everyone asking if she's still got it. I needed to do something."

"You brought him back before that review, so what the fuck was going on?"

Andrea shakes her head. "I heard her rehearsals in the past few weeks. She hasn't been like she always was. I could tell she was too distracted, too focused on other things and not on this tour."

"Too happy? Why the hell did you have Jonah bring me onto this job in the first place if Michael was your righthand man in managing Mia?"

Andrea groans, like all of this questioning is a hassle for her. "I had to do something to show my daughter I was the one in charge. So Michael got a paid vacation for a few weeks, and Mia had to fall in line. You were the perfect man for the job."

"Until we started to care for one another."

"It was only a matter of time before the critics began writing their reviews saying she's lost it. She used to have fire in her soul before, but now those critics are hearing what I heard for weeks. That's what love does to a person. It makes them weak. Mia's career is built on her angst, so I had to make sure a plan was in place."

Her admission that she's had this kidnapping waiting in the wings for just the right time stuns me. "You had to make sure she went back to being unhappy. Christ, you are a monster. And here I thought you were the good one in that house."

Then I remember the stalker letter. "There's never been a stalker, has there? That was all you and Michael, wasn't it? All to whip up sympathy for Mia and keep her in the news. More angst and suffering."

Andrea arrogantly nods, like any of her behavior is something she should be proud of. "Yes, and that stunt did just what it was supposed to do. It kept everyone talking about her, and it helped keep her in the public eye so people would buy more of her music."

"Your daughter walked around in utter terror after every one of those letters. How could you do that to her? You have no idea what it feels like to think someone is lurking around every corner, stalking you and you have no way to stop them."

Again, she waves away my concern for Mia. "She was never in any real danger. My daughter's a survivor. I knew she'd be able to take it."

And then one last mystery solves itself as I stand

there in disbelief in front of her. "It was Michael who shot me, wasn't it?"

That makes Andrea uncomfortable, and she moves away from me toward the door as she stammers, "Tha-that was a mistake, and I am truly sorry about that. I never told him to shoot you or Mia. He was just supposed to follow you two that night."

"How? How did he follow us? We were in your car," I ask, stunned at what she's just admitted on top of everything else.

"All the vehicles at the estate are tracked. I had to do that once Mia got her license. If I didn't, then she might take off and I'd never be able to find her."

Taking a step back, I shake my head at how evil this woman is. "You fucking LoJacked your own car and never told Mia. Jesus Christ, Andrea."

"Stop acting like it isn't done all the time. It's perfectly normal, especially when you're dealing with someone like Mia."

"Someone like Mia? You talk about her like she's a pet who might get away or like she's a performer in a circus you have to keep in line. Your little friend Michael shot me and could have hit her that night with that bullet. Did that ever occur to you when you sent him out to follow us?"

"He got out of hand. I'm afraid he got a little jealous when he saw you with her. But you're obviously all right."

I point at my right arm and explode, "He fucking shot me! What makes you think that jealousy of his won't rear its ugly head and make him shoot her? Tell me where she is, Andrea. I need to get her away from him right now!"

She moves to run out of the room, but I grab her by the arm and yank her back, throwing her onto the bed and her new clothes. Staring up at me in utter terror, she sobs out the address where Mia's being held. It instantly imprints on my brain, and I run out of there to get Drew and Jack.

Just give me a little time, baby. I'm coming for you. I promise.

CHAPTER NINETEEN

ia

SOMETHING'S HAPPENED. I DON'T KNOW WHAT, BUT something's changed with Michael. In the past hour, he's started acting strange, like all the cockiness he was giving me before has disappeared for some reason.

Instead of sitting in that chair across from me and smirking like he's the king of the world, now he's pacing back and forth in front of me and looking nervous. Worse, he's waving his gun around like he's expecting to have to use it on someone soon.

Using a much softer voice than before, I say to him as he walks over near a wall of boxes, "Michael, whatever happened here, this doesn't have to end badly. I don't know why you did this, but we're friends. We have been for years. I can help you put an end to whatever you're doing here so neither one of us gets hurt."

He merely shakes his head but says nothing to me. Worry looks like it's been etched deep into the lines in his face, especially around his mouth. Instead of smiling like before, now he frowns and mumbles something about people not being able to be trusted.

"I know how that can be," I say, seizing upon his aggravation with people in this world who say one thing and do another. "Sometimes you feel like you can't believe a thing people say, right? I feel that way too, Michael. It's okay."

Some part of that upsets him, and he whirls around with his gun in his hand and waves it angrily in front of my face. "It's not fucking okay! I did everything she ever wanted. Every fucking thing! It didn't matter how ugly it made me feel. I did it because she said that was the only way I'd get what I want. Well, this ain't what I ever wanted. That's for sure."

Confused, I try to think of something supportive to calm him down and make him see I'm not the enemy here. Whoever is screwing him over is. I don't know why he keeps saying she. Maybe he's getting me mixed up with whoever his partner is.

"I know you did, Michael. You were a good friend to me. You really were. I'm sorry you got fired for helping me run away to that hotel. That wasn't right. I never wanted you to lose your job over that."

He stops in front of me and stares down into my

eyes, making me think I'm getting through to him. So I keep talking, hoping he'll untie these ropes and let me leave this place.

"I'm sorry about a lot of things. You deserved better than to be let go like that. I can talk to my mother when I see her and we can figure out some way to fix this. You just have to let me go, Michael."

Shaking his head slowly, he finally says, "You have no idea about anyone around you. Do you realize that? You think I'm angry about getting fired. Andrea never fired me. If you weren't so stupid, you'd check the payroll when someone gets fired to make sure they don't keep getting paid. The only thing that happened was my job location was transferred from the estate to my apartment."

Now it's my turn to shake my head. What is he talking about?

"I don't understand. My mother fired you. She did that without even asking me, but she did it and brought in a new head of security. What are you saying? That you're still getting paid? For what?"

In a flash, he looks like the man who taunted me for hours earlier today. Smiling broadly, he laughs and sits down in that chair of his across from me. He holds the gun over his head and sighs heavily.

"No wonder she thought you were so easy to manipulate. You really are. You're so busy being lost in your life and your music that you don't pay attention to a damn thing. Andrea has kept paying me because she had things for me to do. Things only I could do because I'm the one who's been with her for all this time doing her dirty work."

A terrible thought races through my head. "Are you saying you and my mother are together?"

When I accused my mother of using Michael as an errand boy that night at the pavilion, I said that out of anger. Was I closer to the truth than I even understood? Have they been sleeping together?

"If you're asking if I'm fucking her, the answer is no. Not that I'd say no, necessarily, since I know she's got money, but that's not what Andrea and I are to one another. She's my boss. I work for her. I do what she tells me to do."

None of what he's saying makes sense. My mother fired Michael after I ran away to that hotel because he made the reservations for me. She blamed him for that stunt of mine, as she called it.

"I don't know what the hell you're talking about. You got fired for helping me run away. Are you claiming my mother knew the whole time where I was because you two were working together?"

Laughter explodes out of him, and he throws his head back. "Knew? Of course, she knew. I told her everything. I reported back to her whatever you told me. When you said you wanted to get away, I let her know. She was the one who suggested I reserve that room for you. What makes you think my sister could afford five hundred dollars a night on her credit card? I told you Aimee barely made rent most months."

I close my eyes as tears begin to sting the back of my eyes. My mother knew and still created that media circus with them analyzing and dissecting my entire life on TV while she held press conferences looking like the devastated mother of a missing woman?

"Why? Why would my mother do that?" I ask, not sure I want to know the answer.

"Because that's what she considers her job to be. She's your manager, so it's her job to keep your name in the public eye. She wants you to be on the front of every tabloid and the first story on every entertainment show around. That way the money never stops rolling in and her gravy train keeps on rolling down the tracks. You're the gift that keeps on giving, Mia. She realized that the first time you ran away back when you were sixteen. When she saw what the press did when she told them the news that you were missing, she saw what a goldmine your diva stunts could be. So she instructed me to tell her whenever you were planning anything so she could make the most of whatever shit you pulled."

When he finishes, I open my eyes as the tears stream down my face. "No. I don't believe any of this bullshit. My mother loves using the media as much as the next person, but she wouldn't stage manage me that way. She's my mother, for God's sake!"

My pathetic attempt to defend her makes him laugh even harder, but I sense a type of mania has taken him over, like he knows he's not going to get out of this the way he planned. I get the feeling he's going to hurt as many people as he can, whichever way he can.

All I can hope is he doesn't shoot me.

"You want stage managed, little Mia? Try this on for size. I told you she gave the orders and I carried them out. If she said to mail a letter to you, I mailed a letter to you. If she said follow you, I followed you. If she said make Mia disappear for a few hours so she can alert the media and crank up the sympathy machine for poor little you, I made you disappear by taking too long on whatever we were up to. Sometimes it was a hotel. Other times, it's a factory like this one."

What does he mean mailing a letter to me? Then it all becomes crystal clear what he's saying. My mother hasn't simply used my behavior to our advantage with the media. She's created chaos and problems that I had nothing to do with to keep what he calls the sympathy machine for me running at full steam.

"You're the stalker? So I never really had a stalker? She's had you sending those letters to me for three years. Those letters terrified me. The two of you saw how scared I'd get every time I'd receive one, and still you kept sending them?"

Michael shrugs. "All part of my job. Andrea thought a stalker would help keep the public's focus on you when you were getting ready to go out on tour, so every time, she'd have me mail a letter. Just one and that was it. And it did the trick. Even this time with your new security guy right there. Made the entire house go into a tizzy, I think is how she described it."

The most horrifying thought of all fills my head as I watch him happily describe his dirty work for my mother. "So I've never been in any danger but she knows you're holding me here, tied to a chair, with a gun pointed at me?"

Nodding, he says the words that break my heart. "She set this whole thing up."

"Why? The tour is going great. The audiences are loving my shows. What's behind doing this now?" I ask, wishing I could stop crying but the tears won't stop coming.

My questions seem to irritate him, like he's tired of explaining how evil he and my mother have been. "I'm not really sure what her motives are this time. She did say something about reviews of those Tampa shows being in the shitter, but I think it's also to make your new security chief look bad. At least that's why I'm doing this."

"Why do you two want Liam to look bad? What has he done to either of you?"

Before he can answer my questions, a noise like a door opening on the other side of the factory makes him jump up out of his chair. With his gun aimed to shoot, Michael looks back at me and shakes his head.

"Don't make a sound, or I swear to God, someone's going to get hurt."

As he disappears behind the wall of boxes, I know he's beyond reason now, so all I can do is pray that sound was Liam and his men coming to rescue me. But what if it's his partner?

No, his only partner is my mother. My own mother who cares only about the media circus she's created to ensure public sympathy keeps my record sales climbing higher and higher and she gets wealthier and wealthier.

Shaking my head, I try to stop myself from crying and start thinking clearly. If I call out for help and he shoots the person before they can reach me, then I don't know what he'll do in retaliation to me. But if I don't let whoever is here know where I am, he might get the jump on them and shoot them.

I have no choice. I have to hope whoever made that noise is here to help me and my calling out to them is what they need.

"Help! I'm back here! Behind the wall of boxes! He has a gun!" I yell as loudly as I can after hours without a sip of any liquid passing my lips.

No one responds, and I listen for any clue that someone has come to save me. Suddenly, a gunshot pierces the silence, and my heart skips a beat that it may have been Michael shooting Liam.

Then I hear his voice and it's like I can breathe again.

"Michael, you need to let her go! Do that and nobody has to get hurt. Don't and I'm going to make sure you get what you gave me on the street that night, except I won't just graze your right arm."

Oh, my God! Michael shot Liam? Did my mother order him to do that too?

"I'm not going to jail because that crazy bitch thought this was a good idea. No way, man! There's only one way out of this, but I'm not going out alone!" Michael yells in a panicked voice.

I swivel my head right and left to see where he is because he means he's going to take me down with him. Oh, God! Liam has to stop him!

"Don't hurt her," Liam yells, his voice closer this time. "I'm warning you. Don't hurt her."

A second later, a gunshot from behind the wall of boxes a few yards in front of me makes me jump in my seat. I wait to hear Liam's voice, to hear him say even a single word so I can know he's okay, but there's nothing.

"Liam!"

All I need to hear is his voice. "Say something! Say something so I know you're not hurt!" I cry.

Holding my breath, I wait to hear something for what feels like an eternity. My heart slams into my chest like a jackhammer, and all I can think about it how much I need him to be alive.

Please, God. Let Liam be safe. I love him, and he loves me. Don't take him away. Please.

"Liam! Liam! Please answer me!"

Still I hear nothing.

Frantically, I scan the part of the factory around me for some hint that he's still alive, and then I see the most beautiful sight in the world when he runs around that wall of boxes and spots me.

"I'm here, Mia. It's okay. I'm here."

He rushes over and crouches down in front of me to untie my ankles and then my hands as I silently thank God for letting him live. I fall into his arms, relieved but still terrified that this isn't the end of this nightmare.

"I got you, Mia. It's okay. I got you."

My sobs overwhelm me as everything that's happened replays in my mind. "I thought he shot you. I thought you were dead," I say, my tears making my words sound all disjointed.

"I'm okay. I came as soon as I could. You're safe now."

All I want to do is forget everything that Michael and my mother have done. But will I ever be truly able to do that?

Liam holds me to him, whispering in my ear, "I'm so sorry, Mia."

In his arms, I feel safe and protected, but I can't help but ask what happened with Michael. "Did you…?" I can't finish that sentence. I don't want to. It's too horrible to think my mother's stunt ended with someone losing their life.

"He's gone, baby. I didn't have a choice. It was him or me."

My mother's to blame for Michael's death, not him. Whatever it takes to make the world understand that, I'll do it because he doesn't deserve to pay for her crimes.

Leaning back, Liam looks up at me and gently wipes my tears from my cheeks with the pads of his thumbs. "I'm sorry it took me so long to get here."

I think I know why, but I have to ask. "Did she try to stop you? My mother is behind all of this. She's behind the stalker and Michael kidnapping me. And I guess she was behind him shooting you too."

With a nod, he says, "I know. She admitted everything."

"I'm so sorry, Liam."

That gets me a big smile, and he asks, "What are you saying you're sorry about? You didn't do anything wrong."

Looking down into those beautiful blue eyes of his, I let out a heavy sigh, so happy to be with him again. "I'm sorry I didn't pay attention and I didn't listen to you when you said I needed to be more careful. If I hadn't fought you every step of the way, this may have never happened."

He cradles my face in his strong hands and smiles. "Your mother is to blame for all of this. Not you, Mia. So don't blame yourself. You trusted her, and she betrayed you. Nothing more than that."

I close my eyes and let that truth sink in. My own mother betrayed me. The woman I credited all these years with being at my side every step of the way on my rise to the top betrayed me.

And for what? I don't understand it. I would have never fired my own mother, no matter how much she got on my nerves.

Now I want nothing to do with her. I never want to see her again.

Liam eases me up out of the chair I've sat in for hours, holding me so I don't fall. I turn to look up at him so worried about me being able to take a step and know no matter what happens, this is the man I want by my side.

"I love you, Liam."

He leans down to kiss me, and breaking the very last rule he's held on to until now, says sweetly, "I love you too, Mia."

The coming days aren't going to be easy for either of us, but we have each other. And love.

CHAPTER TWENTY

iam

MIA CLUTCHES MY HAND TIGHTLY, WRAPPING HER fingers around mine as I pull the car up to the house. After what happened in Miami, we've had to deal with my being arrested for shooting Michael, the fallout from her mother being arrested for kidnapping her own daughter, and the postponement of a month of dates on the tour so Mia can recuperate from all that she's been through.

Two weeks into resting up, she heard me talking to my mother about my grandmother's birthday party out at her house and asked if she could come with me. So now, she's squeezing my fingers tighter than a vice and staring at the house while I let the car idle.

"We don't have to go in. Trust me. My grandmother will have more than enough family here to wish her happy birthday, and I completely understand if you're not ready to meet the rest of the Jackson and March clan. They can be a lot, and after what you've been through, nobody would blame you for bowing out of a get-together like this."

Her grip on my fingers loosens a little, and she turns to look back out the rear window. "No paparazzi. I guess even they feel bad for me."

"Everyone should feel sympathy for you, Mia. What your mother and Michael did was horrible."

With a tiny smile, she says, "It seems like a terrible waste of a day free of the media to not go inside for the party."

"Are you sure?"

With her typical sincerity, she nods. "I can't wait to meet your family, Liam. I guess I'm just feeling like I don't have one anymore. My father hasn't been around forever, and now my mother is gone too. It's a little scary."

"I get that. For what it's worth, my family has no problem taking in new people. We're sort of like a cult, except we don't do anything really terrifying. Just a lot of family get-togethers. So many parties. You have no idea what you're signing up for with these people."

She smiles at my attempt at being funny, so I lean over and kiss her softly on the lips. "Seriously. It's your call. Everyone will understand, and even if they didn't, it wouldn't matter because I would."

Her smile doesn't return when I lean back, and she lowers her gaze to look down at our hands. "Are you sure nobody blames me for what happened? You got arrested, Liam."

I slide my fingertip under her chin and gently lift her head so she can see my face when I say, "Nobody blames you. It's okay."

"It's not okay. You lost your job. You love being a bodyguard, but now that you've been arrested, it's all gone. All because of my mother. And your friends got hurt and Kip may never get back to work again. None of it's okay," she says sadly.

"Nobody blames you. You didn't do this, Mia. Everyone here knows that. And as for my being a bodyguard, I'm still protecting the only person I ever want to guard for the rest of my life. But if it's too soon to be hanging out with a houseful of people, you say the word and we're out of here. We can go wherever you want."

Mia takes a deep breath in and lets it out slowly before turning to look at me. "Okay. I want to go in. I've heard so many stories about your family that I want to meet them all. I was just worried that they all think I've ruined your life."

I pull her to me to kiss away that crazy thought. "You didn't ruin my life. You're the woman I love. I did what I always hoped I would if someone I loved was in danger, and I'd do it again. Anyone who knows me isn't surprised that I did everything I could to protect you."

"You're going to want to temper that I'd do it again talk when you go in front of the judge next month,

Liam. Judges aren't famous for being incurable romantics, honey."

"I will, but that's not the truth. I'm not sorry about what I did to protect you, Mia. I love you. You're the best thing in my life, so why shouldn't I have shot the man who was holding you hostage?"

She smiles and taps me on the tip of my nose. "I think you might be the most stubborn person I've ever met. I love you, but you're stubborn, baby."

I can't believe my ears. Mia, the woman who fights me on everything from the moment we met, thinks I'm stubborn?

"I guess it takes a stubborn person to know one?" I ask with a chuckle.

Mia shrugs and turns to open her car door. "I'm headstrong. There's a difference."

As I get out and walk around to her side of the car, I can't help but laugh. "Exactly what would the difference be?"

She stands up, and I close the car door behind her while she walks away. "Headstrong is positive. Stubborn is just stubborn," she says with a giggle.

Turning back to look at me, she says, "I can't wait to see your mother again. She included the sweetest card with those flowers she and your father sent, so I want to thank her in person for saying such lovely things when I needed it most."

I take her hand in mine and bring it to my lips to press a kiss to her knuckles. "I love you. If this gets too much, just give the signal and we're out of here."

"Don't worry about me. I'm going to be okay. I love big families. Remember the Bradys?"

She's right. She will be okay. I plan to make sure of that.

MY FATHER PULLS ME ASIDE ON THE BACK PORCH OF my grandmother's house as Mia tells my mother, Shay, and Olivia about the time she met Elton John. They look like they're hanging on every word that comes out of her mouth, as if she's giving them the secret to a long life.

"She looks like she's doing all right. How about you?" my father asks in a low voice.

"I'm fine, Dad. My attorney thinks the D.A. down there isn't really interested in going through with this whole thing. I'm sticking with self-defense, so if it goes to trial, he thinks the jury will see things the way I do."

"You have enough money to cover things? I know you're going to tell me you don't need any, but your mother and I were talking and since we've taken care of Wilder's legal problems more than once, we think it's only right that we do the same for you."

The sincerity in his eyes that look so much like mine makes me smile. He wants me to know no matter how much he's done for my younger brother that he hasn't forgotten me.

But my father doesn't have to worry that I feel that way. Wilder is who he is, and I'm who I am. I don't blame my parents for wanting to help their kids in any way they can.

"I'm good, Dad. You and Mom don't have to worry. I have the money you guys gave me when I turned twenty-one, and Mia's got money. We're good."

His eyes open wide at my mention of Mia. "So it's a we're thing? Any plans I should know about?"

Turning to look behind us, I see my mother grab onto Mia's arm as she tells them all about how some singer invited her to co-write with him for his next record. "Well, I think Mia's going to be doing a song with some guy, but for the life of me, I can't remember his name. By the way Mom is reacting, I'm guessing he's a big deal."

My father elbows me and laughs. "Everything about Mia is a big deal to your mother. She tells every person she comes in contact with that you and Mia are together. I'm thinking she's going to start approaching strangers to tell them soon."

"She is a big deal," I say as I watch her charm the women in my family now that my grandmother has joined the group.

"So about those plans? Anything you want to give me advance notice of?" my father says in a low voice.

I know what he's getting at, but Mia and I aren't ready to go there yet. Maybe someday, but for now, we're just taking things one day at a time.

With a shrug, I try to be as noncommittal as possible, even though I know whenever I talk about Mia and me looking casual flies right out the window. She's everything, my entire life, and I can't hide it. That's how it is when you're crazy in love with someone.

"Nothing yet, but if anything happens, I'll make sure to tell you and Mom first."

My father leans in next to my ear and whispers, "Tell me first. Your mother always gets the news in this family before me. For once, I'd like to be the one who knows before she does."

Shaking my head, I laugh at how funny my father can be. "Okay, Dad. If and when there's any big news about Mia and me, you're the first member of our family I'll tell."

Just then, Mia turns around to give me a smile and mouths, "They are so into this story!"

What they're into is her, and I can understand why. I've been crazy about her from almost the first day we met.

Well, maybe a couple days after that. Those first days, she just drove me crazy.

Next to me, my father says in a low voice, "You look happy, Liam."

I nod, unable to stop smiling as I watch the woman I love enchant my family just like she does her fans. And me every day.

Turning to face him, I shrug. "I am. I never thought I'd get to have what you and Mom and everyone else seemed to find, but somehow in all the madness in Mia's life, I found something incredible. Someone incredible, Dad."

My father smiles like he's just heard the best news of his life. He puts his arm around my shoulders, hugging me to him, and says in my ear, "You deserve it. I always wanted to see you this happy. It's been all your mother and I hoped for you."

He looks over toward where Mia and my mother are standing, the two of them smiling like they're the best of friends. "She fits in pretty well with this family, I'd say."

I smile at his observation. "It's all she's ever wanted in life—a big family. I warned her to be careful what she asked for. This family can get to be a lot sometimes, but she loves the idea of all of you guys."

"Just wait until the first time we all show up uninvited or it's your turn to host the holidays. Then she'll know the real truth of what a big family is like."

I turn to look at him, curious about his mention of the holidays. "So are you, Cassian, and Stefan handing off the baton to the next generation when it comes to Thanksgiving and Christmas? Have you told Cade, Cash, Alex, and Wilder yet?"

He shrugs, but I can tell he's thought about it. "You're all grown up now. It's time for you boys to take over. I'm not sure how Stefan feels about that since you know he's the king of Christmas, but I wouldn't be surprised to hear Cassian say he's willing to see the baton be passed on. And when you all start having kids of your own, it'll be only right."

Startled by his mention of any of us having children already, I hold my hand up to stop him from going any further with that discussion. "Whoa, Dad. What makes you think we're having kids already? None of us are even married yet."

In his typical Kane Jackson fashion, he levels his

gaze on me and frowns. "Your mother and I weren't married before we had your sister, Liam. People don't have to be married to have children."

The way he says that makes me sound like some out of touch, judgmental asshole, so I quickly answer, "I wasn't saying that. All I was saying is I don't think anyone's planning on having kids yet."

And a second later, across the porch I hear my mother squeal with utter joy. "Who's having kids? Oh, that would be the best news ever!"

From out of nowhere, everyone stares at me like they expect to hear some huge secret I've been hiding. Shaking my head, I try to calm my mother, aunts, and grandmother, but it's no use. They start talking about how they can't wait to have grandchildren and great-grandchildren like it's going to happen this afternoon.

Cade and Alex throw nasty glares in my direction, and Cash walks up to me looking like he wants to punch me in the face. "What exactly do you think you're doing? It's not bad enough they're always asking when we're all getting married? Now you throw having kids into the mix? What the hell were you thinking?"

Mia looks over at me helplessly as my mother and Olivia gush about how wonderful having kids is and I try to think of a way to put this genie back in the bottle. "Cash, don't look at me. I didn't mean that. My father was talking about passing the baton of the holidays to our generation and mentioned when we have kids. Nobody meant now."

"Man, just for that, I'm going to make sure every

time we're all at one of these get-togethers that I ask when you and Mia are getting married. Brace yourself because your mother looks like she might go over the moon every time I bring it up."

Cade hears him threaten me and chimes in with his own promise to make my life miserable from today on. "And if he doesn't, I will. What did you say at the last family party? Payback's a bitch. You better believe it."

I look over toward Mia to see if she's angry with me too since I doubt she's thought about us having kids already, but she looks utterly content to listen to everyone talk about children and our big family growing. She gives me a tiny wave and beams a smile before turning back toward the people around her.

At least one member of the Jackson-March clan isn't pissed at me.

A few minutes later, she rushes over to me and excitedly says, "Your mother, aunts, and grandmother are taking me inside to watch some video of you in a school play. They say it was the cutest thing and I have to see it. Oh, Liam, please tell me you don't mind because by the way they've described it, it sounds wonderful!"

Beside me, my father says beneath his breath, "Sixth grade end-of-year play where you were the coach of the baseball team, and you had that huge speech you gave your players."

Trying not to cringe at that memory, I force a smile and nod at her. "I don't mind. Just don't expect award winning acting."

Mia throws her arms around my neck and kisses

me on the lips. "I bet it's going to be the cutest thing ever! Your grandmother mentioned she has pictures of you from when you were a little baby all the way up through high school too."

I should have expected this today, but now that the women of my family have decided to break out all the Liam memorabilia, all I can do is shrug. "Try to remember the early teenage years can be rough on a kid."

"You're so humble. I bet you were the most handsome thirteen-year-old around."

My cousins all break out into laughter behind me as my father snickers. Some family they are. Did I go laughing when Cade first brought Hailey around or when Cash brought Savannah here for the first time?

As Mia runs off, I turn around and throw them all dirty looks. "Can't a guy catch a break with you people? It's not bad enough she's about to sit through that terrible play?"

Cade slaps me on the back and laughs. "Dude, I wouldn't worry. She's clearly not going to be swayed by Grandma's school play video."

From across the porch, Hailey calls out to him, "Honey, we're all going inside to see the videos your grandmother has of all you guys. If you or Cash are looking for me or Savannah, just give us a yell, okay?"

Both my cousins' expressions fall, and now it's my turn to laugh. "Not so funny now, huh? Cade, remember you being a sad elf in that Christmas play in first grade? Grandma does. And Cash, I seem to recall you being a toothbrush in a third-grade school play for Dental Health Week. Good times, right?"

Now the only one laughing is Alex, but he shouldn't count himself safe yet. "Laugh now, man, but wait until you bring someone here for the first time. It won't be so funny then."

Still enjoying our misery, Alex shakes his head and smiles. "First off, unlike the rest of you, I didn't have any awkward years, so Grandma can show whatever she wants. But more importantly, I'm going to be single for as long as I can be, so you'll be waiting a long time for this guy to be bringing any woman here. I think I'm going to head in and take a look at these videos. I need a good laugh."

That makes all of us roll our eyes. "Dude, that's like the exact line the guy says in every movie right before he falls head over heels for some beautiful woman as she's rushing out of some office building and slams a glass door into him. He falls to the ground, and when he realizes what happened, he looks up at her and it's game over. He's in love," I say as he shakes his head while my other cousins agree with me.

"What happened to you, man?" Alex asks like he's disappointed in me. "Now you're as lost as these two," he says, pointing at his brother and best friend.

"It's inevitable," my father says with a chuckle. "You can try to fight it, Alex, but what's the point?"

A look of horror crosses my cousin's face. "The point is that I like being single."

He pushes past me and heads toward the steps

down to the beach. "And I don't plan on that changing anytime soon!"

When he's gone, I turn to Cade and Cash and nod. "Oh, yeah. What's Grandma always say? Methinks he doth protest too much? Something tells me Alex isn't as single as he claims to be. It's only a matter of time, gentlemen. It's only a matter of time."

With a chuckle, Cash whips out a hundred and places it on the table. "I bet he's off the market within two months."

Cade pulls out his wallet and lays his hundred on the table between them. "I'll give it three. He's going to fight it, but he'll give in. What about you, Liam?"

I think about it for a moment while I fish my bet out of my pocket. Placing it on top of theirs, I hum to myself. "I think I'm going to take six months on this one. He's stubborn, and I know something about that. Six months and he falls like a ton of bricks."

My father laughs as he walks away to go inside the house. "I don't know how long it will take, but something tells me when Alex there falls, it's going to be hard, like Liam said."

Smiling, Cash taps the pile of money. "The countdown begins today. Whenever it happens, I think your father's right. Alex is primed to go down hard."

I look out toward the beach and see him sitting alone on the sand drinking a beer. It wasn't that long ago I thought I'd be single forever. Here's to hoping he finds someone as wonderful as I did.

CHAPTER TWENTY-ONE

ia

WHILE LIAM FINISHES HIS CONVERSATION ON THE phone with Kip, I change out of the sundress I wore to his grandmother's house today and into the sexy lingerie I bought with Ainsley last weekend. Black and lacy, it's exactly what I wanted to surprise him in tonight.

After she found out all my mother and Michael had been up to, my life coach came around to seeing how wonderful Liam had been this whole time. When she told me about how she sat him down and told him he better not break my heart, I couldn't help but hug her for being a true friend.

Of course, when Liam heard her version of that conversation, he had to laugh. It seems she didn't tell the entire truth about that day in the dining room. Or maybe she just saw their talk differently. It's no big deal, though, now that my best friend and the man I love aren't mortal enemies anymore.

Twirling around in front of the mirror, I take a good look at myself in my new teddy and smile. Perfect for the man who has everything.

At least, that's the way he describes his life. I don't agree. Because of what happened with Michael, Liam can't be a bodyguard anymore. He claims he doesn't need the money and there's only one body he wants to guard now anyway, but I worry he's going to end up missing the job he loved so much.

As for my mother, well, she calls me dozens of times a day with hundreds of excuses for all she's done, but I'm not ready to forgive her yet. Eventually, I will, though. She's my mother. What choice do I have?

"Well, Kip is feeling much better. He says…"

In the mirror, I see Liam stop dead two steps into our bedroom, his mouth hanging open. I guess this black lacy number is as wonderful as I thought, after all.

Turning around to face him, I smile. "You were saying about Kip?"

Wide-eyed, Liam shakes his head. "Kip? Who's Kip? I don't know any Kip."

"Stop making jokes. How is he?" I ask, giggling at how cute my man can be.

Liam's mouth turns up in a big smile as he walks over to take me into his arms. "Kip's doing better. He said to tell you thank you for all you've done to make sure he's got the best doctors taking care of him. Now, what's this about and who do I thank for it tonight?"

I look up into those beautiful blue eyes staring down at me in utter appreciation and love how he still gets moony-eyed over me. "This is a little surprise I bought especially for you, and you can thank me any way you like."

When he kisses me, I feel like I'm the luckiest girl in the world to have Liam as the man who loves me. To think I couldn't stand him in the beginning.

Well, for like a day. I'm not blind, and I'm not stupid either, contrary to some people's opinions. I know a great man when I see him standing in front of me, even if he was far more stubborn than I thought I could ever want.

He leans away and sighs. "I plan on thanking you all night."

"Then this teddy was money well spent. I told Ainsley you'd love it."

Liam rolls his eyes and jokes, "And she said then burn it?"

I give him a love tap on his chest and step around him to walk over to the bed. "Don't pick on poor Ainsley. She sees the error of her ways now and thinks you're great for me."

Behind me, he says, "The life coach finally comes around. The world can return to spinning on its axis once again."

Suddenly, a wonderful idea comes to me, and I spin around to face him. "Oh, my God! I just had the best thought! Your cousin who looks like the other one who's with Hailey? He would be perfect for Ainsley, don't you think?"

Liam stops and shakes his head, as if he needs to immediately remove that thought from his brain and shaking his head fast is the only way to do that. "Alex? No. Trust me. In fact, I can't imagine anyone who could be more wrong for him than Ainsley. Sweet Jesus, no."

His answer to my fantastic suggestion makes me scrunch up my face. "First of all, some woman who smells like onions all the time and has warts all over her face from being cursed by an evil warlock would be more wrong for Alex, and second of all, he'd like her. She's beautiful, and he's got a real mellow thing going with him that she'd love. They'd be perfect together."

Horror fills Liam's expression with every word I mention about Ainsley being the woman for his cousin. "No, they wouldn't. Alex is mellow in a way that has nothing to do with Ainsley and her Zen business. He's more like the kind of cool that comes from having everything he could possibly want in the world, and that includes women, money, and anything else. That would not work for your friend. Trust me."

Baffled by his discounting my truly wonderful idea, I ask, "Why? Ainsley is very sweet, and she's proven herself to be a great friend."

He takes a step toward me and wraps his arm around my waist to pull me to him. Shaking his head again, he answers, "She's clingy as all hell, Mia. She didn't like me because I was intruding on her turf. I know you know that."

Disappointed, I nod. "I guess. She is beautiful, though. He'd like her. I just know he would. I want her to be happy like I am."

Liam gently pushes my hair off my face and kisses me sweetly. "I know, and that's why you're a great friend, but Alex isn't the man for her. My cousin enjoys his life with whatever women he chooses to date. She'd never want to be part of that harem. She could barely deal with not having you all to herself. Imagine how she'd be with a man."

Pouting, I sigh and accept he's right. "Okay. No more matchmaking for me, I guess."

He dips his head to nuzzle my neck just under my ear and whispers, "Now let's get back to this surprise you got for me. Any chance you're not going to be upset when I take it off?"

Sometimes he can be so cute.

I look up at him and smile. "That's the point of it, honey. Women wear these things expecting they won't stay on for long."

As he slides his hands up under the teddy to cup my ass, he smiles wickedly. "Good because I'm thinking it'll be off you in about five seconds."

My gaze rolls over his body still covered by clothes. As I begin to fiddle with the first button on his gray dress shirt, I say, "You know, that's some big talk from a man who's still fully dressed."

Opening up his arms out to his sides, he chuckles. "I'm all yours. Do what you want to me."

My fingers get stuck on the third button down. Grimacing, I look up at him and say, "What I want is to get this shirt off, but it's like these buttons are entirely against us making love tonight."

In a flash, he pulls the shirt up over his head and throws it onto the floor behind him. Grinning, he says, "Next problem?"

I slide my palms over his broad chest and down his chiseled abs until my hands come to rest on the top of his pants. "I do love a man who knows how to take care of business."

"Then I'm the man you want."

Tilting my head back as my fingers easily open the button on his pants, I take in the beauty of him. God, he's even more gorgeous than he looked the first time I saw him without a shirt.

"Is it possible you get more stunning every time I look at you?" I ask and then slowly pull down his zipper.

"Probably not," he says as he cradles my face in his strong hands. Liam presses a soft kiss to my lips and whispers, "I think that's what they call the haze of love."

I stare up into his gorgeous blue eyes that make me feel like I could get lost in them. "Maybe. Whatever it is, I love it almost as much as I love you."

"Even though I'm stubborn and as by the book as they come?" he asks with a sly grin as he slides his hands down to the bottom of my new lingerie.

Before I can answer that question, he slides my

teddy up my body and says, "Arms up. It's time for this to retire for the night. It's done its job."

While I shimmy against the lacy fabric as he lifts it up over my head, I joke, "If I could use my arms, I'd check. As it is, I'll have to take your word on that, Mr. Jackson."

Liam tosses my brand-new black lace teddy on top of his shirt on the floor before guiding my hand to the front of his pants. "No need to take my word on it. Take his. He's ready to go."

I watch him strip out of his pants and underwear and ask, "Why do men always refer to their bits and pieces as he?"

When he finishes and he's standing naked in front of me, it feels like something has stolen my breath away. The man I adore is like a Greek god come to life, and he's all mine.

As I slide my hands over his chest, he answers in a way that sounds almost innocent, "I think it might be strange if we called them she. She's ready to go? Go where?"

He really is so cute sometimes.

Liam takes me by the hand and leads me over to the bed. When he sits down on the edge, it reminds me of that night we watched The Brady Bunch together and how I was crazy about him even then.

"Mia? Is something wrong?"

His question pulls me from my memories, and I shake my head. "No. I was just thinking about that first night when I came to your room, and we watched my favorite show. Were you wearing gray sweatpants that night?"

I gently push him down onto the bed as he shakes his head. "I don't remember. Why?"

"Because you look great in gray sweatpants."

He pulls me to him, kissing me hard like he wants me to know the time for talking is over, but then he smiles and says, "I thought women loved all guys in gray sweatpants."

As I straddle his hips, I shake my head. "Not all. It's female kryptonite, but gray sweatpants can only do so much. On you, of course, they're like your superpower."

With one slow thrust, he pushes into my body, filling me completely. Smiling up at me, he runs his tongue over his bottom lip, leaving it glistening wet.

"I like this superpower better," he says with a moan.

I roll my hips and sigh. "Mmmm...I agree. This one is the best."

We make love like it's the first time, like we can't get enough of one another. Liam is everything I've ever wished for in a man but never thought I'd get. He's sweet and sexy, tender yet gruff, and even his insistence on doing things by the rules charms me now.

But none of that matters when I'm in his arms and he gives me what every woman wants. True love, mind-blowing orgasms, and the security that whatever comes tomorrow, he'll be there to protect me.

His arms wrapped around me, he sighs after that

first round of sex as we lie together in the bed we share in our house. It used to be my house, and I made sure to fill it with as many people as I could so I'd never be alone.

Now it's our home, and I have all I could ever want right here with him.

That's what the song I wrote that night in New Orleans is all about. I know when the world finally hears *Safe In Your Arms* for the first time that how I feel about Liam will come through loud and clear. It'll be my biggest hit yet too.

Even more importantly, I know when he finally hears it, he'll know it's my song to him.

My head on his chest, I think about our time at his grandmother's house today and sigh in utter contentment. "I loved being with your family today, Liam. Every one of them is now my new favorite person."

He presses a soft kiss to the top of my head, and when he speaks, the sound comes from deep inside him and makes his chest rumble beneath my cheek. "I'm happy you had fun. They loved you, just like I knew they would."

"You don't really hate having a big family, do you?" I ask, my voice trembling in anticipation of his answer.

Liam stays silent for a long moment but then answers, "No, not really. They can be a lot sometimes, but I can't imagine my life without them."

"Do you think you might want to have a big family someday?" I whisper against his skin.

He doesn't take long to answer that question, thankfully. "Yeah, I think that would be great."

I lift my head off his chest and look at him, happy to see him smiling. "Me too."

It's only been a few months since we got together, and I have a tour to finish and a million other things to do, but all I can think about at this moment is how much I want to spend the rest of my life with him. Maybe it's crazy because I'm so young. Maybe we should date for longer.

I don't know. All I know is after spending time with his family today, I truly felt like I had finally found a home.

"You got quiet there, all of a sudden," he says. "Something on your mind?"

I could say the words right now and see what he thinks. Maybe it's not too soon. But then I look into those beautiful blue eyes of his and see how much my old-fashioned guy would want to be the one to say them, so I shake my head.

"Just thinking about the future. That's all."

Liam gently pulls me back down to rest against him and sighs. "I love you. We can deal with the future tomorrow. Tonight, let's just be Liam and Mia, two people crazy about each other."

He's right. Tomorrow is good enough for the future. Tonight is for us.

"I love you, Liam."

With his arms wrapped around me, I feel safe like I've never felt before him. Now only one thing could make my life perfect.

I hope someday soon that big family of his will be my family too.

ALEX MARCH'S DUET, SENSUOUS AND DESIROUS, IS COMING SOON! PREORDER YOUR COPIES TODAY AND BE READY WHEN IT GOES LIVE

ABOUT THE AUTHOR

K.M. Scott writes contemporary romance stories of sexy, intense, and unforgettable love. A New York Times and USA Today bestselling author, she's been in love with romance since reading her first romance novel in junior high (she was a very curious girl!). Under her Gabrielle Bisset name, she write paranormal and historical romance. She lives in Pennsylvania with a herd of animals and when she's not writing can be found reading or feeding her TV addiction.

Be sure to visit K.M.'s Facebook page at **https://www.facebook.com/kmscottauthor** for all the latest on her books, along with giveaways and other goodies! And to hear all the news on K.M. Scott books first, sign up for her newsletter today and be sure to visit her website at **http://www.kmscottbooks.com**

BOOKS BY K.M. SCOTT:

Crash Into Me (Heart of Stone #1)

Fall Into Me (Heart of Stone #2)

Give In To Me (Heart of Stone #3)

Heart of Stone Volume One

Ever After (Heart of Stone #4)

A Heart of Stone Christmas (Heart of Stone #5)

Return To Me (Heart of Stone #6)

Forever With Me (Heart of Stone #7)

Heart of Stone Volume Two

Hard As Stone (Heart of Stone #8)

Set In Stone (Heart of Stone #9)

Silent As A Stone (Heart of Stone #10)

Heart of Stone Volume Three

All of Me (Heart of Stone #11)

Temptation (Club X #1)

Surrender (Club X #2)

Possession (Club X #3)

Satisfaction (Club X #4)

Acceptance (Club X #5)

Complete Club X Series Box Set

Sweet Things (Dirty Boss #1)

Private Secretary (Dirty Boss #2)

Play Date (Dirty Boss #3)

Dirty Boss Volume One

K.M.'S BOOKS ARE IN AUDIOBOOK TOO!

www.ingramcontent.com/pod-product-compliance
Lightning Source LLC
Chambersburg PA
CBHW020607180626
46810CB00007B/2681